Amish Vows:

Amish
Renegade

By Rose Doss

Book 1

ISBN: 9781983036132

Cover images courtesy of Willard and canstockphoto
Cover by Joleene Naylor.

Manufactured/Produced in the United States

CHAPTER ONE

Kate Beiler clutched at the small, warm hand of the girl she'd raised since her marriage, numbness gripping her as they stood facing the plain wood coffins in front of her. It didn't seem possible that her dad and mom were gone.

Around them, the community stood silently listening to Bishop Yoder consigning the remains of the loving couple into God's care. The bearded men stood around the two graves with bowed heads; the strings of the women's prayer *kapps* fluttered in the chill air and all Kate could think was a bizarre random observation that it should have been raining. The chilled wind gusted crackling, dry fallen leaves around her feet and she hoped little Sarah was warm enough in her black stockings and skirts. The freshly dirt from the freshly dug graves smelled damp and the heavy clouds overhead had been dark gray all day. Kate closed her eyes on the thought that they too should weep. Her own cheeks were again wet with salty tears and she wondered inanely if a person could grow moss like the dark rocks near the random brooks that trickled along the fields.

They'd always been there for her—*Mamm* and *Daed*. Even through the dark days when she'd been so conflicted about *rumspringa* and Enoch. Not saying a negative word when she'd angrily married Jakob Beiler so suddenly upon coming home from her visit to Uncle Brandon in the *Englischer* world. After Jakob's sudden death several years later from a fast-moving cold, they'd lovingly welcomed her and Jakob's child, Sarah, into their home.

1

And they'd known. Known that her marriage to Jakob hadn't been all rosy. Known even that she had questions about this life in which she'd grown up.

Bishop Yoder's prayer went on and on as the damp cold crept up her legs and Kate knew she should be listening.

Still in the daze that had held her since that knock on the door had heralded the beginning of this nightmare, she drew in a tight, damp breath and wondered what had happened to the broken remains of the carriage in which her parents had died.

Down the row of mourners—past her best friend, Hannah and her husband, John, stood Enoch Miller, his dark felt hat clutched between blunt fingers.

Kate idly looked at Enoch's hands, still tanned from summer work, and wondered how long she and Sarah would be allowed to stay in the house.

She'd always known that her father farmed rented land, but it hadn't ever really seemed important. Not till now that she and Sarah had no home.

Closing her eyes in silent prayer, Kate again beseeched God to help her know what to do. They had no place to live and Sarah had no one else. Jakob's family lived several counties away and, after his death, they had been very comfortable leaving his daughter in her care. They all had big families themselves and in addition were caring for Jakob's aged, failing parents.

Only now what? Not a day ago, Daniel Troyer had appeared on the weathered porch of the wooden house that had always been home to her father and mother, announcing that she and Sarah needed to vacate the house soon after the funeral because he was now old enough to take over and farm his father's land.

Kate didn't know what to do. She'd had an increasing inner conflict with some parts of the Amish lifestyle and the restriction on the roles allowed women, but feeding and housing little Sarah was the pressing problem of the moment. After Daniel Troyer's visit, Kate had sat down at her mother's aged writing desk and written in desperation to her maternal uncle. Maybe she and Sarah could stay with him, just till she figured out what to do. Uncle

Brandon was an *Englischer*, but he'd always supported his sister as having the right to live as she pleased.

Only Uncle Brandon hadn't responded and Kate didn't know where else to turn.

As usual, thoughts of Uncle Brandon brought memories flooding through her of the tortured time she'd spent at his home on the ill-fated *rumspringa* that had brought an end to her and Enoch. Enoch with his dark hair and dark eyes… Enoch who smelled so wonderful and who she'd loved so madly when she'd grown old enough to start attending the young people's Sunday evening sings. Courting with him, his warm lips clinging to hers, falling deeply in love with Enoch…and quarreling with him so many times.

Several hours later, Kate sat on a hard chair in the kitchen of the house where she'd grown up, a plentiful spread of simple foods, steaming and fragrant, on the table. Even if she'd wondered how it would be to live a broader life, this part of her world was comforting and warm, the coming together of friends whenever help was needed. She loved so much about the Amish life. Sitting numb with little Sarah still on her lap wearing the same dark clothes as she wore, Kate knew Hannah must have scrambled to pull together the meal for the bishop and his family and the friends of her parents, Elizabeth and James Lehman.

Feeling another salty tear seep out of the corner of her eye, Kate reached up to wipe it away. It wasn't considered necessary— or even desirable—for emotions to be visible when God recalled a loved one. She knew that grief was considered private, but this hiding of emotion had always been difficult and seemed foreign to her. Tipping her head back to stare sightlessly at the ceiling, Kate ached for them both, for her kind father and for her mother, who'd so loved him that she left the *Englisch* world to join James in his Amish life several years after she finished college.

Across the simply furnished room, Enoch sat with several other men, his features somber, his black jacket strained over the broad shoulders she'd one clung to as he kissed her senseless. He and her *Daed* had stayed friends—even after she and Enoch had broken things off. It always startled her that no woman had snatched up Enoch after all these years. She'd been caught up trying to be a conformable wife to Jakob and learning to be a mother to young Sarah, but she'd never lost her stifled feelings or the *ping* that came with being in Enoch's presence. She could still remember the cottony texture of his shirt over his muscled arms as he swept her into silly play.

She'd prayed about it, knowing that with marrying Jakob after returning from the *rumspringa* she'd denounced all interaction with Enoch. He'd cut her off after she went on *rumspringa* against his wishes and she'd moved on. She no longer had any right or need for a reaction to Enoch Miller. That was in her past now. She'd wrestled with her response to him, just as she fought with herself about her doubts. There were parts of the Amish life that rankled her still—that women weren't allowed any role in the church, but were limited taking care of the home and having children. Frustrated that these doubts—and her attraction to Enoch—continued even after joining the church and marrying Jakob, she'd even talked to her mother about it.

In her gentle wisdom, Elizabeth had often helped Kate disconnect from her misguided passions and she'd hoped her mother could help her move beyond any leftover emotional reaction to Enoch. *Mamm* had always tried to temper Kate's sometimes tumultuous emotional reactions to life, telling her she needed to think before she reacted. Sadly, talking to *Mamm* hadn't stopped her thoughts from returning to Enoch.

Closing her eyes, Kate prayed silently to God to help her learn to make her way without her mother.

When young Sarah wiggled on her lap, she ran a soothing hand down the child's warm back. Now she would continue trying to do for the little girl what Elizabeth had done for her. Give her knowledge; try to respond with rational advice. Settle her childish anxieties or storms. Of course, Sarah was a more calm, easy child than she'd been. What a trial Elizabeth must have found her, even when she'd done so much to help Kate learn.

Sarah was her anchor to some degree. Another reason to stay in this life. The Amish way seemed the best for raising a loving, Godly child. Elizabeth had helped with that, too. She'd considered the narrowness of this life before pledging to Kate's father.

Lost in her thoughts of growing up with her educated mother teaching her after she'd left the eighth grade of schooling considered sufficient for the lifestyle, she didn't realize for a moment that Bishop Yoder stood before her.

"Oh, I'm sorry, Bishop." Kate looked up, the smile on her face feeling mechanical.

The bishop settled onto a wood chair next to her, nodding toward Sarah. "Perhaps the child would like to sit with the other children for a while."

"Of course. Run along so I can talk to Bishop Yoder, sweetheart. I'll see you in a few minutes." She shifted Sarah to her feet.

"Yes, ma'am." The girl wandered off to a corner where several other children sat.

"She's a good girl is Sarah." The bishop watched her go before turning to Kate. "I understand that the farm here and house belongs to Mr. Troyer and that his son, Daniel, plans to take it over."

"Yes," Kate responded, her voice low.

His wispy gray beard brushing against his shirt front, the bishop leaned back in his chair, frowning at her. "Well, have you thought about where you and Sarah will go? Are you planning to seek help from the Bielers? They live several counties away, don't they?"

Looking down, Kate pressed her hands against the black fabric of her apron. "Yes, Bishop Yoder, they do and I don't believe there is a place there for Sarah and myself. I've asked, but Jakob's brothers have their hands full."

"The older brothers have many children." Bishop Yoder nodded. "God has blessed them."

The pit of despair in Kate's stomach seemed to grow. She had yearned for a child, but none had come to her and Jakob. "Yes. They and the other Bieler brothers and sisters—all just getting established—have taken on the care of Mr. and Mrs. Bieler. They're both in poor health, I understand."

"I had heard that." The bishop's voice was heavy as he shifted more toward her. "I know this is hard for you, Kate. The sudden deaths of your mom and dad so soon after Jakob's. What is it? A year now? Who would have guessed they would be gone so quickly? Both so young and vital, not like the older Bieler's."

Tears clogged Kate's throat, making it impossible to respond and she only nodded.

The bishop looked at her for a moment with piercing eyes. "You have to think about the future."

"Yes, Bishop." She swallowed hard. "I plan to look for a job in town. I know there isn't much I'm trained for—"

"Here in Pleasant Township?" His question was abrupt.

"Yes. Here or over at Mercerville. I thought maybe as a waitress or a cook—"

The bishop sat back in his chair, his expression stern. "And where would you and Sarah live? Who would care for her while you work?"

"I'm not sure about those issues," Kate said, trying to ignore the acid ball of desperation in her stomach. "I thought maybe Sarah and I could rent a room with one of the families here."

"Most have no unused rooms. You know," Bishop Yoder started almost before she finished, "my son, Aaron has no wife."

Kate stared at him. "Yes."

"And he has a fine farm a little west of here—with a tidy house on it." The bishop glared at her over the top of his glasses. "He has no wife."

An image of the bishop's youngest thin, sandy-haired son flashed in front of her. "He's—he's barely out of school, isn't he?"

"Four years now," the older man said in a satisfied voice. "He's a man grown. Aaron's eighteen now…and he needs a wife. Just like you need a husband."

"Oh…I don't think I could, Bishop." She stumbled into speech, glancing up at that moment. Across the room sat Enoch between two other farmers who had also sometimes traded work with her father.

Enoch's even brown gaze was leveled right at her as if he were standing before her, hearing the bishop's conversation. Suddenly, Kate felt flushed as if the room had grown much warmer. It was as if her senses woke up—the smell of food from the kitchen mingling with the quiet chatter of friends and relatives that sat nearby.

She made herself look away, saying, "Bishop Yoder, it hasn't been long since Sarah lost her own dad. I just don't know…"

This was certainly not the time, she knew, to mention possibly living with her *Englischer* uncle and confiding her own frustrations with the Amish church to Bishop Yoder was a commitment Kate wasn't ready to make.

The bishop stood, his dark jacket rustling. "Think about it, Kate Bieler. You must act soon and Aaron isn't a bad choice."

"No," she looked down at her hands, "of course not. Thank you, Bishop Yoder."

She couldn't imagine marrying the pimply-faced, younger Yoder son who'd not yet out-grown his gangly stage. For a moment, Enoch's face flashed across her mind and she found herself lifting her head to look at him again. She'd fallen for Enoch when he wasn't much older than the Yoder boy was now. He'd always been broad-shouldered, stocky and anything but pimply, bringing a flutter to her mid-section that even Jakob had never reproduced, much less man-child Aaron.

"I'm sure Daniel Troyer will give you and Sarah a week or two," the bishop finished, "but you must decide soon."

"I know." Kate looked at her lap, swallowing hard. All she could think of was missing her parents horribly, but this reality had to be faced.

She watched the broad back of the bishop as he walked away. Staring down at her hands, fingers twisted in her lap, she fought against the tide of panic rising in her chest. Her parents had often cautioned her to resist drowning in her feelings and Kate knew they wouldn't want her to fall apart now.

"Kate?"

Looking up at the sound of the familiar deep voice, she felt tears flood her eyes. She had no idea why Enoch standing before her made her want to cry.

"I just wanted," Enoch said, his dark hat still between his broad fingers, "to let you know how much I'll miss your *Daed*."

Swallowing in a desperate attempt to quell the sob that rose in her throat, she looked up at him through the shimmering wetness flooding her eyes. "Thank you, Enoch."

As if in response to her distress, he slid into the chair vacated by the bishop. Between their chairs, where no one in the room could see, she felt the brush of his strong hand against the fabric of her dark skirt. Automatically, as if her hand had a mind of its own, she reached down to touch him briefly before pulling back.

"I loved your *Daed*," Enoch said in a low voice. "From when I was just a bump on a log, he took the time to teach me, like he was my own father. My *Daed* remarked on it. And sharing work with him these last four years; your *Daed*'s been a great help many, many times."

"I know," she choked out, reaching up to wipe her cheeks, "that he had the greatest respect for you, Enoch."

"It is a great loss, that buggy accident that killed your mother and him."

Feeling the grief rise up in her again, Kate bent her head. She felt the strings of her prayer *kapp* brush against the front of her dress, but she couldn't stop the loss that flooded through her. Bringing her hand up to shade her face, she wept silently.

Enoch made no remark, sitting next to her as she cried softly.

Flashing a glance at him once her tears had subsided some— her cheeks dried quickly with her hankie—memories flooded Kate. For years now, she'd resolutely refused to allow herself to dwell on

Enoch Miller and she'd managed pretty well. But his kind words coming at this time, swept all her protective barriers aside.

If only she hadn't argued so angrily with him years back when they were both young and in love. He'd made her so mad. *Rumspringa* should only be for boys becoming men, he'd said. Girls had no place *running around* before they committed to becoming members of the church and marrying to settle down and raise families. Before that huge fight, she'd been crazy about Enoch. She'd even confided her darkest thoughts to him as they lie sprawled out in the grassy field. Maybe she didn't totally believe in the Amish life that left women so few choices and gave them no role in the church. Maybe God had another direction for her.

The next morning, having made breakfast for her and Sarah with the feeling still of being in a weird nightmare, Kate stood on the weathered front porch of the house she'd grown up in, confronting Daniel Yoder.

"I know you just buried your parents yesterday, Kate Bieler, but you and the child must find other lodgings." Daniel's words were dogged. He clearly didn't relish throwing them out of their home, but he was just as obviously determined. "The fall crops must be planted, you know. It has to happen now."

The crispness of the autumn air swirled around them and Kate hugged herself against the chill.

Having lived her whole life on a farm, she understood that the seasons didn't stop, even though her world had come crashing down. Perhaps she should have felt guilty for grieving more intensely the loss of her parents than she had Jakob, but she couldn't feel differently.

"Of course, Daniel. I understand the fields must be planted, but the house… Is it so important that Sarah and I leave the house right away? I-I'm still trying to decide what to do."

If Uncle Brandon would respond, she would know if that door was absolutely closed. He'd been kind to her on the ill-fated *rumspringa* she'd defiantly taken when the big argument with Enoch ended their engagement so rudely. All through her weepy, morose month with him, Uncle Brandon hadn't intruded into her distress or tried to direct her choices.

At this moment, she felt so overwhelmed it would have been a relief if someone would tell her what to do.

Daniel cleared his throat awkwardly. "I need the house, too. My wife—I'm married now if you remember—my wife and I have been living with my parents in their house—and we have a babe on the way."

His face looked strained as he spoke.

Forcing a smile on to her lips, Kate said, "Oh, that's right. I'm sorry for not remembering. It's alright."

The young man in front of her turned red. "That must have been around the time Jakob died."

"Yes." Kate nodded, looking down at the rough leather boots he wore. "Sarah and I will be out of here as quickly as I can arrange a place to stay."

"I'm sorry." Daniel Troyer nodded one more time before he left the porch.

She watched him go, her mind spinning uselessly. She knew taking Sarah to Uncle Brandon's—if that had even been an option—would mean carrying the little girl outside the world she'd always known. Jakob wouldn't have liked that, but Kate didn't know what else to do.

The *Englischer* world had seemed exciting, foreign and scary to her all at once when she'd spent that month in Baltimore, at least until the break up with Enoch. Strangely exciting, but not home.

She'd had growing doubts about what life here in the Amish community would mean for her, but with no Enoch in her life, everything there had seemed cold and bare. She hadn't been able to truly explore the *Englisch* life. He hadn't written to her all that month she'd been in Baltimore. Coming home, even more angry at his apparent indifference, she'd lent a defiant ear to Jakob's courtship. He was a widower a little older than her, with a young daughter.

Strangely, enough it hadn't occurred to her to leave the Amish life then. She loved many things about her friends here—Hannah and John—and the simple, hard work felt familiar and comfortable to her.

Her parents hadn't said anything when she announced that she'd agreed to marry Jakob. With fall coming on then, the work in the fields suspended for the winter. It had only made sense to marry quickly.

Jakob had been kind, although maddeningly undependable, but she should have loved him more.

Kate looked across the empty field next to the house, musing that she'd had no trouble falling in love with Jakob's daughter. Sarah felt like her own blood. She could no more have given the child over to the Bielers or the family of the woman who'd died giving birth to her than she could have cut off her own arm. Only now she had no home and no way to support Sarah and herself.

Shuddering, Kate knew she couldn't marry young Aaron Yoder. She knew better than anyone what an unhappy, unfulfilled marriage was like. She'd been down that road before. Both she and Aaron had deserved better.

With a deep sigh, she turned back to the door. She needed to get Sarah dressed to go stay the day with Hannah. Her friend would look after the little girl while Kate looked for work in one of the nearby towns. She could even be a maid at the hotel out on the highway.

A weight pressed down on her chest as the screen door slammed shut behind her in a gust of autumn wind. Maybe this was a punishment for even considering leaving the life God had given her. Maybe Enoch had been right about everything.

CHAPTER TWO

Sitting at the broad table in Hannah's warm kitchen, Kate watched as her friend bent to take a steaming pan out of the gas oven, her solid dark skirt dusting the floor.

"Katie," Hannah swung around to face her, her cheerful face red from the heat, "you must remarry. It's the best option. You know there were no job openings in Pleasant Township or in Mercerville. No one is looking to hire a cook or a maid, although God knows you're a terrific cook."

They'd first become fast friends when they met in school, Hannah an older student of eleven while Kate had just entered it as a six year-old. It had seemed an odd pairing, but as Kate got older, the two had only become greater friends.

As her friend swung back around to the stove, Kate protested, "You aren't actually thinking I should marry Aaron Yoder! That little boy?"

"No," Hannah dropped the hot pads on the counter as two of her children ran behind her, slamming the back door behind them. She came back to sit across from Kate with the peculiar gracefulness found in some pregnant women. "I think you need another husband. You should marry Enoch Miller."

Feeling her heart jump into her throat, Kate stared in shock at her blonde friend. Prayer *kapp* slightly askew with untidy ringlets clustered at her neck, Hannah nodded. "It's the perfect answer."

Hannah reached over to gently rock the aged cradle that sat at the end of the table in a spot close to the warmth, but not too close to endanger the *Boppli* sleeping there.

12

"How can you say that?" Kate exclaimed in a strangled voice, jumpy at the thought of what her friend suggested. "Enoch Miller doesn't want to marry me. Certainly not now. I just need my Uncle Brandon to respond, even if that means taking Sarah into the *Englisch* world. I'm sure Uncle Brandon will help us."

"But you wouldn't be able to keep the Amish ways. That would be hard."

"No, I wouldn't...and that would be hard." Kate looked down at the scarred table top. It would be hard to live something other than the plain life. She'd never told Hannah about her doubts at what she saw as the limits for women in the Amish church. Just her parents and Enoch...and telling him certainly hadn't ended well.

"I'm not sure Enoch doesn't want to marry you, even now. I've noticed him watching you." Hannah bracketed two sturdy hands around the plain ceramic mug in front of her. "You know I'd be glad to have you and Sarah move in here with John and me—"

"Of course not." Kate nodded at Sarah's rounded figure. "With you and John preparing to add a fifth child?"

Her gaze swept around the cozy, homely kitchen. "Your house is already full."

Hannah leaned forward with a gentle smile. "There will always be room for you and Sarah, Katie, but I know very well you wouldn't be happy under the same roof with my John. You two haven't a thought in common. You think I don't know you bite your tongue when he's around? That you're civil to him for me?"

Looking down as warmth crawled up her neck, Kate shook her head. She still couldn't understand how her friend didn't find John Hostetler annoying and irritating, but Hannah clearly didn't. "That's not true, at all. I know you're very happy with John, and I hope I'd be civil to anyone you loved."

"Yes, I am happy with him," Hannah said with a satisfied smile, "and you are civil, but that doesn't mean you and he could live together comfortably."

"What's more to the issue," Kate got up to lift a suddenly wakeful and fussy Lydia from her wooden cradle, "is that you and John are already sleeping three children to a room. I know very well that Lydia's cradle goes into your bedroom. Heaven knows where you'll put the new baby when it comes."

"God will provide," her friend responded complacently, smiling as she watched Kate balance Lydia on her bouncing knee. "You are a good *Mamm*, Katie. You need a good man to give you children of your own. I don't know why God never sent you and Jakob children."

"Neither do I, but Sarah is my own child and I still say that Enoch doesn't want to marry me. Not after I broke off our engagement when we were *youngies*." She absently reached for a small rag to wipe the baby's soft chin. "I just wish God would provide for Sarah and me now. I was so grateful that we had a home with my parents after Jakob died. "

"God provides for those who act to care for themselves in accordance with His laws. I know that while Jakob was alive, you did your best to be a good wife to him. Anyone could see that he was—well never mind. Why, you've always treated Sarah as your own kinder. But I also know that your heart beats a little faster when Enoch is around."

"Don't be silly," Kate knew she sounded annoyed and tried to soften her tone. "Besides, I keep telling you, Enoch and I always argued when we were courting back when we were younger. You know how angry I was at him for telling me I couldn't spend my *rumspringa* with Uncle Brandon in Baltimore. That's why we broke up. You know he never wrote me when I was gone. Never spoke to me directly after I married Jakob."

"Maybe, but a lot of water has passed under the bridge since then. Don't you think there's a reason why Enoch never married? I've seen the girls around here try to get his interest, as much as people don't let on as to who is courting who. Enoch has never wavered." She smiled and nodded at her friend. "He's waiting for you."

Kate stared at her friend, struggling against a flood of emotion. She'd taken the disastrous, impulsive step of marrying in haste. Out of hurt and anger. Her mother had always told her to count and pray before did anything helter skelter, before her impetuous mouth blurted out what couldn't be unsaid. Kate knew her *Mamm* had been right. After fighting so angrily with Enoch before she'd left for *rumspringa*, she'd gone to visit her uncle and ended up watching his mail in Baltimore like the box might catch on fire.

But Enoch hadn't written. All those long six weeks, he'd stayed silent.

She knew he hadn't wanted her to go. He'd lectured her, declaring that girls should stay home, that only boys needed *rumspringa* to sort out whether they were ready for the heavy responsibilities that came with marriage and church membership. She'd angrily reminded him that girls also had to think about the responsibilities of being wives and mothers and obedient children of God, even if the church wouldn't let them take on more important roles. Enoch's insistence that she had no right to go on *rumspringa* hadn't angered her enough; they'd disagreed over the Amish tradition of only educating children through the eighth grade.

But she'd been shocked that he hadn't written to her when she was in Baltimore. Not one word. She'd even written secretly to him once herself, but he'd never replied.

Looking down at the infant she bounced gently on her knee, she flashed back to only a few days before when Enoch had stood stoically beside her parents' graves and later come to the meal at the house. Remembering the strong touch of his fingers on hers when he'd sat beside her while she wept made her breath come a little faster and she hated herself for it.

While she was married to Jakob, she'd secretly— shamefully—been glad Enoch hadn't married. It was a terrible thing, to wish him to be alone when she'd accepted another.

She drew in a shaky breath. "Enoch hasn't asked me to marry him. Not since our courtship when we were *youngies*. What do you want me to do? Propose to him?"

Hannah got up from the table bench, coming around to hold out her hands for baby Lydia. "Yes. I think that's a very good idea."

"Kate won't have my boy," Bishop Yoder sat in Enoch's parlor a week later. "He went to speak to her himself two days ago. I think you should marry her, Enoch. You know Daniel Troyer and his wife are going to have a *Boppli* in the spring? He needs that house and the farm."

Enoch stared at the bishop, so stunned by the old man's words that he couldn't sort through the thoughts in his brain. The first of which was "ah hah! Now I have her where I want her!" There was nothing now between him and Kate Lehman. Not anymore. He'd sent up a silent prayer again, asking for forgiveness at his own relief back when Jakob Bieler had died. He had nothing against the man, except that he'd married Kate Lehman.

Ever since Kate Lehman—he refused to think of her by her married name—had become available again, Enoch had felt more spring in his step. But he didn't want to think about what might come next. That something might come, something more between them. Too many mixed thoughts there.

They'd fought so horribly before she went to Baltimore. His chest had felt tight the whole time she'd been on *rumspringa*, like he might burst.

He'd known she was in trouble after her parents died, but Enoch had thought she and little Sarah would move away to live with one of the other Beilers. He'd even thought she might be given the job of looking after old Mr. and Mrs. Beiler, but that clearly was not the case.

Five years before, Enoch had given his hand and heart to her, but Kate had flouted him, running off to Baltimore on her wild *rumpringa* spree and then coming home to quickly marry Jakob Bieler. Jakob Beiler, of all people. At least, she could have picked a man with a backbone to replace Enoch. Firming his jaw to resist the sneer that came to his face when he thought of her choice, he kept a level gaze on Bishop Yoder, who was still speaking in his dry, precise voice.

Enoch knew he should feel bad about thinking that way about Kate's action. Wishing for Jakob's death had never even occurred to him, but after the farm accident, he'd thought about the horrible irony of Kate's situation. Even her own dad had mentioned it once to him—just briefly, when he was helping Enoch clear the new field in the weeks after she and Sarah moved in with her parents.

She'd rejected him for Jakob Beiler.

"Marrying Kate is the Godly thing to do, Enoch." Bishop Yoder summed up, wiping a hand across the black pant leg that covered his knee. "She and young Sarah have nowhere else to go. They need a home and she needs a husband. As a community, we must provide."

Enoch's younger brother, Isaac, sat silently in a straight-back chair across the room, his face solemn as he listened.

"Why me?" Enoch found himself saying. "There are others…beside myself and Aaron."

The bishop shook his head. "Levi Lapp is still grieving his poor wife who died in childbirth not so long ago and you know the Martin boy is too young, even younger than my Aaron. Everyone else is married…or courting others. Besides, Enoch, you know God did not intend man to be alone."

Bishop Yoder frowned at him. "You have never married. You have no children to help you till the soil. It is not right in the eyes of God."

Enoch drew a long breath and let it out slowly. He'd never denied that Kate was a beauty, even without all the paint and provocative clothes he'd seen on women in the *Englisch* world. A sizzle of something had run through him, just at the touch of her hand the other day, surrounded by others and with her eyes full of grieving tears for her parents.

His hands tightening into fists almost without him being aware—as if his flesh wanted to touch hers. Enoch straightened his fingers out carefully over his knees. He was drawn to Kate and he hated that about himself. He was still mad at her for yelling at him in their *rumspringa* argument and throwing him over for Jakob Bieler after she'd returned from what he didn't doubt was her wild spree at her uncle's.

He'd wrestled with himself all the days she was gone, knowing he had no right to her then. Despite all his attempts to stop her, she'd gone to her uncle in Baltimore. He'd ached to write to her and have her write back to reassure him that she hadn't forgotten him, that she wasn't lost to the *Englisch* world but was coming back to him after all. But his pride held him back. He'd been too angry when he'd gotten her note, thinking to punish her by not writing and maybe to pull her back to him by his silence. And then when she'd finally come back, he'd breathed a sigh of relief. Not all who went into that world came back to the Amish way of life. Some stayed and all the while Kate had been gone, he'd fiercely argued with himself that she hadn't deserved to waltz back into his life after doing Heaven knew what she'd done with other, *Englisch* men.

After she'd so quickly married, he'd told himself to forget her.

"I need to pray about this, Bishop." It was all Enoch could find to say. He needed time to organize his thoughts, time to beat back his anger…and hurt, if he could.

"Of course, Enoch. This is a big decision and it calls for much prayer." The older man got to his feet to leave. "You talk with God about this."

He nodded to the younger man. "Good day, young Isaac."

"Good day, Bishop." Isaac had risen to his feet.

Closing the door after Bishop Yoder left, Enoch turned back to his brother. "Well? What do you think?"

Isaac smiled, reaching over to punch his brother gently on the shoulder. "What does that matter, brother? You are older and wiser. Why ask me?"

"Because you are not a fool," Enoch growled, "That's why. What have you so silently been thinking?"

Isaac settled back onto his chair. "I remember a brother who secretly slipped away to Katie Lehman's house when they were both young. I used to see you from my wood shop. I remember a brother who came back from her house silly from her kisses."

"I meant about now," Enoch said impatiently.

"I remember," his brother went on as if he hadn't spoken, "how annoyingly, sickeningly happy you were when the two of you were courting."

Enoch said nothing, just looking at his brother in silence. He couldn't dispute what Isaac said. Kate's warm, responsive lips had made him silly.

"Of course, when you two were courting, I was just a *Scholar,* too young to know anything of love—"

"And you're so old now," Enoch interjected with a mocking laugh.

"—but I remember how much fun Kate was then. How funny and charming." Isaac smiled. "You know, before she married Jakob Bieler."

"I think you should go home."

Again Isaac went on, "She seemed different when she returned from visiting her uncle right before she married Jakob. Like she was waiting for something—or someone—to welcome her home, but never found that."

"Daed probably needs you for something." Enoch said, not responding to the memories his brother's words evoked. He'd been so angry at her, so relieved that she'd returned. No one knew better than he that Kate had struggled with aspects of being an Amish woman. Her mother, Elizabeth Lehman, hadn't been a typical role-model, with her college education—but Elizabeth had left the *Englisch* world to marry James Lehman. That fact alone should have silenced Kate's rebellious thoughts.

Of course, he hadn't always listened to the wise counsel of his own father, Samuel.

"She seemed sad then, Kate did. When she came back." Isaac looked at him. "Kate's seemed sad for a long time now."

Enoch got up to go to the bright window, flooded with an unacceptable anger at the thought of Kate being another man's wife. He couldn't help the clenching of his fists. She'd been with Jakob for nearly four years and their marriage still rankled. He'd told himself he'd accept the reality of her choices at some point. If she'd carried Jakob's child, she might not have been of any more interest to him. But that hadn't happened for whatever reason.

"I think you ought to marry her." Isaac returned his level look when Enoch glanced back from the window. "You've always liked her. Anyone could tell. You should marry her."

When his brother left, Enoch stood looking a long time at the fallow field out the window. After a while, he went to the stove to cook himself some supper. After leaving his parents' home, he'd gotten proficient at cooking, if not skilled. At least, he'd been able to keep himself alive. Standing at the stove in front of the sizzling frying pan, the heat from the grease wafting up to him, he closed his eyes.

God, I don't know what to do. I still have this anger in my heart for her. But I don't want to see Katie with yet another man— not Aaron Yoder or any other. He also didn't want her seeking a man from another Amish community to marry her and offer a home to her and young Sarah. *She's here, Lord, but for how long? She talked of leaving our life, of seeking out a new world. Do I marry her? Even knowing she may leave? Marriage is for life. Do I marry her, God? Even though You know I have this evil in my heart sometimes and want her to suffer?*

Opening his eyes to stir the frying food, Enoch waited for God's answer. He was all jumbled up inside. The thought of marriage to Kate—and every earthly thing that would mean—sent a surge through him, but he knew it wasn't right. The Bishop said the Godly thing to do was to offer her marriage, but Enoch knew his motives in doing that were ungodly in the extreme. Even though the sight of her grieving her parents had prompted him to offer her comfort, some part of him still wanted her punished for her faithlessness with him. His anger pushed him to take her for that reason alone.

How could he want to comfort her grief and at the same time, want to punish her at the same time?

No Heavenly voice spoke into the silence in his head and his room, though.

The craziness of the situation had her suffering both ways. Either she and young Sarah were homeless or he married her—

which would enable the revenge he'd craved since she'd chosen Jakob Bieler over him.

"But where are we to live?" Sarah's voice was plaintive as she sat on the upturned bucket in the barn a week after the Lehman's funeral.

"I'm not quite sure yet." The warm milk from Bessie's teat streamed into the bucket beneath the Guernsey as Kate performed a task that had long been her job on the Lehman farm. Her father had refused to get the more modern milking machines some of their community owned. "But you are not to worry, Sarah sweetie. *Mamm* will work something out."

"So we can stay here? Living in Papa Lehman's house."

"No, not here." Kate looked at the youthful rounded face of the child that had become her own. Even if her marriage to Jakob hadn't been all roses, she had gotten a lovely daughter from it. "Weren't you going to get some dinner for Bessie?"

Glancing up towards the loft where her dad had kept the hay, she watched Sarah walk over to the loft ladder.

"Sorry, *Mamm*."

"It's alright, *Boppli,* but Bessie shouldn't go hungry just because we aren't sure where we're going to live. Besides, I'm expecting a letter from Uncle Brandon any day. Then we'll be all set."

Sarah disappeared up the ladder, only to poke her head over the rail a moment later. "Here it is, Bessie. Dinner!"

The sweet-smelling hay she tossed over the rail drifted down into a clump on the wooden floor.

"*Mamm*, if your uncle does invite us to live with him doesn't that mean moving away? Wouldn't we be a far distance from our friends?"

Still working the cow's warm udder, Kate thought of kind Uncle Brandon and his sleek apartment in the city. Sarah had no idea how far they'd be from everything they knew.

"Probably. Wouldn't it be fun to travel to a far place, though?" She smiled at the eight year-old. Sarah was the most loving and best child and it only drew her further into Kate's heart that she shared some of the impetuousness and strong feelings that had plagued Kate all her life.

Climbing down the loft ladder, Sarah skipped the last few rungs, jumping down to the floor. "I don't know. Maybe I wouldn't like traveling. Or a big city. My friend, Miriam, went with her family to visit family that lived away and she said she got sick on the buggy ride."

"Well," Kate said, finishing up with Bessie, "Uncle Brandon lives farther away than a buggy ride. We'd probably take a train."

"Oh." Sarah gathered the hay, stuffing it into Bessie's feed box. "That sound really far away from our friends."

In a typical conversational change of directions, she said, "What will happen to Bessie, after we leave this farm?"

"Um," Kate wiped her hands on the course fabric of her dark apron. "Daniel Troyer said he wants to buy all the stock and keep them with the farm."

"Oh," the young girl said again, concluding sadly, "I guess Bessie has a home, even though we don't."

Her mournful words pierced Kate right through the heart and she bent to hug Sarah tightly. "We will, sweetie. We will have a home."

She stared over Sarah's head, her stomach tightening. There was no avoiding what had to be done. Without a response from her uncle Brandon and no job on the horizon, she now had to seriously consider finding herself another husband. It was one thing to carry Sarah away from her Amish community to a safe home with her uncle, but that wasn't to be considered if she had no way to support the child. Even though Kate couldn't completely squelch her own discomfort with some aspects with the lifestyle, she had no other choice…marriage it was. Only not to baby-faced Aaron Yoder.

Kate drew a deep breath. Maybe Hannah was right.

Maybe she should ask Enoch to marry her.

Later that day, Enoch closed the barn doors, pushing against the latch to make sure it was secure. When he swung back toward the house, he paused, seeing the black buggy that had just pulled up. Feeling himself stiffen, he gazed at Kate sitting behind the horse.

As he walked slowly toward her, Kate climbed down from the buggy, shaking out her long skirt and smoothing her dark apron nervously before she turned toward him.

Enoch stood looking at her a moment, his chest feeling tight. He'd done a lot of thinking and praying about the possibilities.

She faced him, her blue eyes darkened by some emotion he couldn't quite read, which was unusual for Kate.

"I need to talk to you, Enoch Miller."

"Alright." The October winds gusted around them, prompting him to say, "Let's go inside. It's warmer."

To his slight amusement, she looked a little startled by this, as if she'd expected to say her piece in his front yard. He led the way up the steps to his wide front porch and she followed silently.

Opening the door to his front room, he held it as she passed him, going inside.

"I don't want to beat about the bush, Enoch," she said abruptly, the words seeming to burst from her.

He smiled, not able to help himself. From the first, he'd always been drawn to her impulsive heart, although he knew she'd often tried to overcome it. He hadn't seen that in Kate during her marriage—her warm, open heart. Of course, he'd kept his distance.

Having announced she was going to be direct, she didn't seem to know what to say next.

Enoch gestured toward the cluster of chairs situated around his crackling fireplace. "Sit?"

Looking startled, as if that hadn't occurred to her, she said, "Yes."

A smile still played around his mouth and he realized with a sudden clarity that he knew what he needed to do. It was as if God had spoken to him, even with his tangled up anger and bitterness that she'd rejected him for Jakob—he should marry her. Kate was in trouble and no matter how jumbled his intentions, he couldn't leave her in a fix.

She perched on the front edge of the chair, clearing her throat. "I need to ask you a favor, Enoch."

Pausing, she seemed to struggle for words. "We never really...talked...after we stopped—"

Reaching up to nervously as if to make sure her *kapp* was straight, she finally went on, "After our fight, when we stopped courting."

"I remember." That time was as clear in his head as was yesterday, not that she'd probably seen it the same way, Enoch thought.

"What is the favor?" he asked, even though he knew. He knew what she faced, but somehow he couldn't make this easy for her.

Kate shifted in her chair to face him more fully. "Enoch, I'm in a bind."

He said nothing, letting the pressure of his silence speak for him.

"Unmarried with a child to support, as well as myself...and now without my parents," she drew in a deep breath. "I—I need to marry."

"Sarah's not your child." He felt compelled to point it out.

With a jerky shake of her head, she rejected his words. "Yes, she is. I've raised her the last four years—since she was just five— and the Bielers have made it clear she's mine."

With an edge of bitterness he'd tried to squelch, he said, "What about your Uncle Brandon? Will he not offer you and Sarah a home?"

She looked down at her hands, knotted together in her lap. "I don't know. I don't think so. He hasn't responded to my letter."

"You asked him? You wrote to him?" The questions shot out of Enoch.

"Yes," she responded with a despairing shrug. "He hasn't responded. I have nowhere else. I've even looked for a job nearby here, but I can find nothing."

Kate looked up with a sigh. "I need to marry. I can find no other way to support Sarah. The money my father left has dwindled and I must give up the farm to the Troyers."

Turning to him clearly hadn't been her first solution. Pushing aside the anger that roiled in his stomach at the thought, he said slowly, "What exactly are you saying, Kate? How does this have anything to do with me?"

He knew why she was there. Why she'd opened this subject to him and he wanted to marry Kate. God knew, he'd only wanted her to be his wife. But Enoch also saw no reason to make this easy for her. Maybe she needed to squirm a little, to suffer just a shade of the bitterness and grief he'd felt since she turned away from him.

The dark-haired woman across from him pulled back a little, as if he'd slapped her instead of asking a simple question.

For a moment, he thought the impetuous, emotional Kate he'd known so long ago was going to get up and storm out of his house. Then she seemed to gather herself. "I'm asking you to marry me, Enoch."

For several long seconds, Enoch didn't respond, his dark eyes staring at her. Kate felt her cheeks grow hot with embarrassment. In all her wrestling with herself at the thought of making this request, her greatest fear was that he no longer had any interest in her. Not allowing herself to cry, she lifted a hand as if to halt the rejection she feared was coming. "Never mind. I can see that the thought never crossed your mind. Forget I was here. Forget I said anything."

Never having felt this embarrassed or shamed before—not even when he hadn't written her on *rumspringa*—she rose to her feet.

He got to his feet, as well. The two of them stood tensely facing one another in his living room like angry bulls in a pasture.

"You know what marriage to me would mean?" Enoch's dark gaze seemed to bore into hers. "That I consider marriage a lifetime commitment and that it would mean being joined together...in all ways."

Halted at his words, a sudden image sprang up before Kate's eyes and she had to close them quickly. Opening her eyes, she looked up at him. "Yes. Yes, Enoch. Let me remind you that I have been married. I do know what it means."

A wry smile coasted over his normally unreadable face. "I wasn't referring to the, er, more intimate parts of marriage, Kate, but to the lifelong commitment of it. Remember, we've talked of your questions. Your doubts about the workings of the church."

Still looking at her with an intense, almost angry expression, he went on, "You are prepared to let go of your questions and commit to my life here? I am a plain and simple man and you know what marriage to me would mean. I want no other life than this service to God. Certainly not the *Englischer* life your uncle offers."

She could only look at him, knowing her feature reflected her thoughts, hating that her turmoil and emotions could be read on her face. "I married Jakob, didn't I? Don't you think that says something?"

He shook his head. "I don't know what that means. I just know all those years ago you could hardly wait to run from me to *rumspringa* with your Uncle Brandon in the *Englisch* world."

Although her own heart was thundering, he almost seemed unmoved by the topic of their conversation. Annoyed maybe.

Kate could only resist the urge to clear her throat again and say in a sharp tone, "Since you asked, I still have moments when I think our faith is confining, particularly to women, but—yes—I do know what marriage to you would mean."

Glaring at her, Enoch said as if she hadn't responded, "It means a life at my side, bearing my children, working the land and going to church meetings. You're saying this is what you want?"

She'd married Jakob Bieler and promised to do all those things... She had done them. Although he was a man who hadn't followed through on his commitments, hadn't inspired her and certainly hadn't left his daughter and her well-provided for, she had nothing to regret...

Except that she hadn't loved Jakob. She tried hard to do so, never turning him away or failing to offer him comfort when he struggled, but Jakob hadn't made her heart beat fast at just the sight of him. From the day they'd married, she'd always done her duty, but she still felt badly that she'd never managed to love Jakob as more than a brother.

Kate lifted her chin as she met Enoch's gaze. Her shortness of breath and the giddy sickness in her belly at the thought a life with Enoch only strengthened her feelings of having failed Jakob, but she knew she had to move on. She had to make this life work.

"I know what marriage to you would mean, Enoch, and I'm asking you to marry me."

As if compelled, Enoch took a step closer to her. The back of her skirt brushed against straight-back chair next to the fire, her hand clenched together at her sides. In front of her, he lifted his hand and slowly reached out. With deliberation, keeping his gaze locked with hers, Enoch brushed his hand along her cheek.

The effect was instantaneous. It was as if a jolt ran through her the moment his flesh had touched hers and she thought saw an answering leap in his dark eyes.

"You want," Enoch said, "you want to be my wife, Kate? To lie beside me, bear my sons? Help me toil the soil and spend your life with me? Even though you sometimes feel the pull of the *Englisch* world?"

Kate's gaze lifted again to his. "Yes. Will you marry me, Enoch?"

CHAPTER THREE

"I'll help you make your dress for your wedding. You don't have much time," Hannah said with satisfaction a day later. "I saw some nice violet fabric at the store when I was there last."

She stood at the ironing board erected next to her hearth, occasionally setting the heavy flat iron on its stand over warm coals.

"No, Hannah. You have enough to do." Standing at her friend's sink washing their family's breakfast dishes to ease Hannah's load, Kate protested, "I have the dress I wore when I married Jakob. It still fits."

"You don't want to wear that dress when you marry Enoch," her friend said in a scolding voice. "You've been wearing it on Sundays for the past five years. Besides, you know the wedding dress must be new."

"I don't see that it makes that much difference." Ever since asking Enoch to marry her, the jitters hadn't left Kate, huddled in her stomach. Yes, her most pressing problem of a home for Sarah and herself seemed to have been solved, but everything that the marriage meant weighed on her. He'd said yes to her proposal, but she'd gotten a very distinct impression that Enoch was still really mad at her.

Even though he'd been kind after her parents' death.

She felt such a fluttering in her midsection and she knew nothing was clear between them, even if he had agreed to come to her rescue.

"It must be a new dress. You know that." Hannah went on cheerfully. "And sitting down to help you stitch it will be no hardship for me. Do you still have black boots? It's a blessing that this has all happened at the close of the harvest. This way you can get married in the wedding season."

"Yes, I have black boots." Talking of the details of marrying Enoch seemed strange, particularly with all that had happened between them. It hadn't always been the case. In years past, before they'd broken up over her taking *rumspringa*, she'd dreamed of setting up house with him.

"Tell me," Hannah drove the heavy iron over a wrinkle, "why did you ever marry Jakob? It seemed so sudden. I knew you and Enoch had been courting. You'd let a few things drop about that, but you said nothing about that when you got back from your *rumspringa*. You and I have been friends since you started school, but you didn't seem to want to talk about marrying Jakob."

Kate made a face. "I know, even though you've always been my wiser, older friend, from the time I was small. I don't know. I guess after coming back from spending time in Baltimore with Uncle Brandon, I didn't really want to talk to anyone about my decision with Jakob."

Hannah went on with her ironing as Kate again plunged her hands in the soapy water in the sink. The older woman said, "I knew, of course, that you and Enoch quarreled. I can't imagine why you quarreled over your *rumspringa*. It's every Amish child's choice—a time to see the outside world before deciding whether or not to commit to our life."

"It was more than a quarrel." Kate set a heavy mixing bowl aside. "We—we ended things. Broke up over it. He was so bull-headed, so crazy about me not going."

"But you did go. To Baltimore."

"Yes." She hadn't seen why she shouldn't. Kate still hadn't a clue as to why Enoch had been so determined for her not to. He'd said that only boys had to decide whether to stay with the Amish life, since they'd bear the greatest burden. Looking at her pregnant friend pushing the heavy flat iron back and forth over her husband's work shirt, Kate smiled ironically. The argument had been even more confusing since Enoch was the only one besides her parents in whom she'd confided her frustrations with the limitations of their life for women.

She'd grown up in a tiny family, compared to the size of most in the faith. Her mother had just never borne another child.

"I remember being surprised that you came back from Baltimore, joined the church," Hannah mused, "and the elders published that you and Jakob were marrying. I know we don't generally talk about courtships, but you and Jakob were really a secret."

"I know." Kate rinsed a plate in the clean water. "We hadn't even talked much before Baltimore. Then when I came back from Uncle Brandon's—Enoch hadn't written me once and didn't seem excited when I came back."

Kate shrugged, the jumbled thoughts in her brain falling out of her mouth. "I kept watching the mail while at was at Uncle Brandon's...but nothing came. I was hurt. Enoch seemed so nuts about the whole thing before I left and then when I went, it was like he'd completely written me off. Like he felt nothing for me."

Hannah looked sympathetic. "That must have been hard."

"I was hurt. And Jakob was...smitten with me." Kate rewashed a plate she'd been holding. "I guess I was feeling...bruised after Enoch and Jakob seemed nice."

She smiled wryly at her friend. "And Sarah was a sweetie. A poor, motherless, orphaned girl, all mouthy and annoying at that age. I just fell for her."

Looking up from the shirt she was carefully ironing, Hannah placed the heavy iron on the stand. "So you married Jakob in order to be Sarah's mother?"

"Not totally. Like I said, being adored by Jakob seemed like a wonderful thing when Enoch was such an angry bear."

"And then you married Jakob." Hannah looked at her steadily. "You were angry, too."

"Yes, and my parents tried to caution me to slow down, not to jump into marrying, to give it another year, but I...didn't listen."

Shaking her head, Kate started drying the dishes. "I was so hurt I didn't listen."

"And you wish you had? I know all wasn't wonderful when you were married." Hannah looked up from her ironing to flash Kate a compassionate look. "It wasn't anything you said. You just seemed…unhappy, except about spending time with little Sarah."

"Don't be silly, Hannah." Kate kept drying the dishes. Even though he was often difficult, she still struggled with not having been able to truly love Jakob and the truth felt so shameful she'd never spoken of it. Not even to her mother, although her parents had also guessed she wasn't a happy bride. After Jakob's death, they'd once mentioned that parents always knew when their kids were unhappy.

"You've been married many years, my friend." Kate looked over at her. "You know no marriage is always wonderful."

"This is true," Hannah confirmed, drawing her husband's shirt from the ironing board, "but I would guess it will certainly be different to be married to Enoch than it was to be married to Jakob."

The older woman gave her a meaningful smile.

"Hannah!" Kate put her drying cloth down to send her friend a scandalized look before she broke into laughter.

Her friend's smile widened wickedly. "I've been married awhile, Katie. I'm not dead. Enoch is a very attractive man."

Kate looked beautiful, her hair as black as a raven's wing, peeping out from under her black bridal *kapp*, and her eyes so blue Enoch could only think of them as having the same vivid color as the darkened sky before a storm. And he didn't even want to think about the sizzle that had gone through him at just the touch of her hand.

As she greeted their wedding guests a week later in Hannah and John Hostetler's parlor, Enoch tried to ignore the unaccustomed feel of the bow tie around his neck and the thundering of his heart.

This was a big step, marrying Kate.

As jumbled up as he felt about her, he knew what he wanted. From the time he'd seen her growing up so sassy and beautiful, he'd been drawn to Kate. Then when they argued before she went off on that awful *rumspringa* and then come home to marry Jakob, Enoch had hated being drawn to her. Even though he knew it was a sin, he'd hated her.

Enoch wondered still if he were doing the right thing. At least Katie and little Sarah would be safe in his home, though, even if he had mixed motives. The racing of his heartbeat when he thought of Kate as his wife was familiar. He remembered it from the kisses he'd stolen when they were youngies in love. His body's attraction to her hadn't changed.

"Quit pulling on your bow tie," Isaac reminded him with the glimmer of a smile from the chair beside him.

"Well, doesn't yours feel like it's choking you?" his brother asked gruffly, keeping his voice low as he cast him a sideways look. "I have no idea why men have to wear these things when they get married."

Shrugging, Isaac leaned against the wooden back of his chair. "Tradition I supposed. Like women wearing only blue or purple dresses. Lots of Ordnung ordained wedding rituals."

"Don't get too smug about it, brother," Enoch recommended. "You'll be marrying soon."

"I hope so," Isaac responded serenely. "I'm just waiting for my Rebecca to get a little older."

"Let's hope all goes well with that," Enoch said, remembering a simpler time when he'd known that he and his Kate would marry and build a life together. He wasn't the type of man to worry a lot and he hadn't given much thought to her *rumspringa* until after Kate had confided her doubts. Then, he'd grown less matter-of-fact about her time in Baltimore. The outside world didn't offer him any temptations. He'd grown up here on his father's farm and, although he'd spent a short time in the *Englischer* world as was expected, he'd never had any question that this simple life of worship and soil between his fingers was for him.

Kate's mother, being college-taught herself, had made sure to educate young Katie well beyond the necessary in the Amish world. Enoch himself had been relieved to finish eighth grade and have school behind him. It didn't take much for a man to know how to study his Bible and read to his *Bopplis*. Enoch had grown up in a big farming family. He hadn't wanted anything more.

Until Kate.

The Hostetler home had been filling around him with community and wedding celebrants since early that morning and the rooms were now growing full. Soon he knew the Bishop would take Kate and him into another room to counsel them on the responsibilities of married life in God's eyes. While they listened quietly to his counsel, Enoch knew that their friends and relatives would crowd into the house and sing hymns.

The length of the wedding service—prayer, scripture reading and lengthy sermons—had never seemed like a chore to him before, but this day stretched out before him like an eternity. He knew that after they were married, he and Kate would spend the afternoon and evening visiting with their friends and relatives. He knew, too, that they were expected to bed down in one of Hannah and John's crowded bedrooms in order to help with the clean up the next day. Nothing should be left for their hosts to tidy before their worship day.

It would be long, long hours before he and Kate went back to the home they would now share with the child of Jakob Bieler.

Enoch wrestled with a surge of hot anger in his chest. To take into his home the child of a man he'd considered his sworn enemy—to even have a sworn enemy—that wasn't a good thing and he knew it. A few years ago he'd had to sit at a wedding celebration very similar to this and watch Jakob's simpering smile as Kate had married the man. Enoch had tried to subdue his rage at the thought. He'd prayed often to God to forgive him, to take the anger from him.

The irony now was that Jakob was dead…and Kate would be Enoch's Frau, after all.

The child she loved so much, who had Jakob Bieler's blood in her, he was now swearing to shelter. He had no idea why Kate and Jakob had never had *Bopplies* of their own. Even though God had told them to go forth and be fruitful, not all women bore children. Kate's mother had only had her.

He knew Kate loved the child, Sarah, like her own. Enoch also knew he could take his rage out on the girl and few would know. He would know, however, and he recognized that it was a Heavenly prerogative to visit the sins of the father on the children…not his.

He could no more be unkind to Sarah than he would ever be to any other child. No matter whom her father had married. That didn't mean he felt very fatherly toward her.

Kate sat in her hard chair placed next to Enoch's, the bishop launching into the closing comments of the third hour of his sermon. In just a few moments, she knew she and Enoch would be called forward by the bishop for questioning. It was the time in which she and Enoch would make their vows. Sparing a moment from her attention to the bishop to glance at the man she was marrying, Kate reflected again on the questions she'd had about their way of life.

She'd never spoke of these to Jakob—not after spilling her heart so openly to Enoch when they were teens and so in love. Not after Enoch had ended up rejecting her so harshly.

"Enoch Miller," the bishop intoned, "step forward. You, as well, Kate Bieler."

Taking a deep breath, Kate did as she was requested, standing next to Enoch in front of Bishop Yoder. Before when she'd been in nearly this same situation, her heart had been sore and filled with anger. She'd known Jakob loved her, but she'd only been filled with a sick kind of triumph.

Acutely aware now of her broad-shouldered groom—nothing like the man she'd married the first time—she again pinned her gaze on the bishop.

"Enoch Miller," Bishop Yoder proclaimed before the packed room, "do you promise to remain with Kate until death? Will you be loyal and care for her during hard times and sickness, as well as good times?"

Not even looking her way, Enoch said in a deep, calm voice, "I will."

Turning in her direction, the bishop repeated his question, "Kate, do you promise to remain with Enoch as his wife until death? Will you be loyal and care for him during hard times and sickness, as well as good times?"

Not nearly as stoic as he appeared to be, Kate flashed a glance upwards at Enoch. So much was still between them, but she knew she had little choice. The thought of being Enoch's wife made her breath tight in her chest. He made her both cold and hot. Could he ever forgive her for marrying Jakob? Nothing ahead of her was sure, except that marrying him was her best choice...and it felt so stupidly right. How could this be so? Was she foolish to marry him now?

Then little Sarah's image flashed before her mind's eye and Kate once again put aside her doubts and fears, saying, "Yes, I do promise."

The bishop then reached forward, taking the couples' hands in his. Kate was aware of his dry, papery hold pressing her hand into Enoch's. "I wish you the blessing and mercy of God. Go forth in the Lord's name. You are now man and wife."

The rest of the day passed in a blur of friends and visiting. Enoch reminded himself that he and Kate would be most likely given a spot in the kids' bedroom at Hannah and John's crowded house, since Kate and the child had moved here briefly. The Troyer boy had taken over the home her parents had rented.

Laughing as she chattered with a gaggle of female friends over by the crowded kitchen hearth, Kate almost seemed like the girl he'd fallen for all those years ago.

"Son!" Joseph Miller appeared at Enoch's side, clapping a hand on his shoulder. "I hope you will be very happy and have many children to fill up your empty house."

Enoch shook his head in wry amusement. "Father, you of all people know this isn't going to be a smooth road."

Joseph leaned against the wall beside Enoch in the crowded room humming with happy voices. "Since when does God ask us to only take easy roads? You and Kate always had strong feelings for one another. Your mother and I knew that when you were youngies."

A laugh rumbling in his chest, Enoch agreed. His amusement dying away quickly, he reflected on just where their strong feelings had taken them. "She's my wife now."

"Yes, my son." Joseph's kind voice matched the look in his dark eyes. "She is that. Before God, you took your vows."

"It's a bad situation she was in." Enoch didn't know why he felt the need to stress this. "With her and the child relying only on her parents...and then them dying. The bishop was clear she needed a home and he told me again that I need a wife."

His father leaned closer. "That's only the way it evolved, Enoch. You and Kate have unfinished business. This is good, the two of you coming together."

Enoch knew the look he threw his dad was sarcastic. "So the Jakob Bieler and the Lehmans died just to force us to deal with our unfinished business?"

Pushing slightly against his arm, Joseph shushed him. "You know God better than that, but He works miracles and uses the wicked ways of this world for His own good. You and Kate are married now...as you were headed toward years back."

Enoch reached for the cup he'd left on the table beside them. "Yes, only now I'm housing Jakob Bieler's child."

His father's gaze swung around to look at Sarah's blonde head. "And she's a fortunate girl. You will be a good father."

"I am not her father." The low words came fast.

Joseph smiled at him with affection. "Not yet, my boy. Not yet."

"Here, Hannah, sit." Kate saw a chair against the wall become empty as the chattering group of friends shifted around them and pressed her friend into it. "You've been cooking and standing on your feet all morning. I will get you a plate of food."

"There's no need, really."

Ignoring the protest, she said, "You rest here. I'll be right back."

Negotiating her way slowly through the clumps of chattering people in the dusky light of many candles, Kate found herself face-to-face with Isaac Miller. Some years younger than Enoch, she'd known him all her life despite them having run with different crowds.

"Hi." It was silly, but she felt a little shy. When she and Enoch had courted years back, she'd spent a fair amount of time at the Miller home.

"Kate!" Isaac stuck out his hand, taking hers warmly. "This is such a great day. Welcome to the Miller family!"

Feeling herself flush as she smilingly accepted his gesture, Kate remembered how startled she'd been when Uncle Brandon had welcomed her on that ill-fated *rumspringa*, pulling her into a hug. She just hadn't grown up with a lot of hugging. Physical affection with children was one thing, but Amish tradition didn't encourage adults to be physically affectionate.

By shaking her hand, Enoch's brother was clearly demonstrating his welcome. "Thank you, Isaac. I appreciate that and I want you and your whole family to come to dinner with us soon."

"That would be wonderful." With the impish smile still playing around his lips, he leaned closer to say quietly, "And may I bring our friend, Rebecca King?"

Kate didn't know the Kings very well, but she'd seen Rebecca sitting in groups that usually included Isaac. "Of course, I'd love to get to know her better."

Isaac beamed. "Thank you, Kate. Here. Would you like me to clear a path through this crowd?"

Laughing in response to his silliness, she shook her head. "It's unnecessary, but thank you."

Hours later, when the guests had slowly left after the day of celebration, Kate busied herself with cleaning, gathering the plates for yet another washing as they started putting Hannah and John's house back in order. Across the room, Enoch, Isaac and some of the other men moved chairs and shifted the room back to its regular set-up.

As she'd told Enoch when she asked him to marry her, Kate knew about the physical aspect of marriage. Despite never having any of her own, she'd learned long ago how babies were made. A girl didn't grow up on a farm without recognizing those realities.

None of that, however, calmed the jitters in her stomach now. She was married to him and from now on she'd sleep in his bed.

Coming to help dry and put away the dishes, Hannah stood beside her at the kitchen sink, lit candles in holders on either side of the sink. She said, "Now John and I want you and Enoch to treat this house as your home. That's why there was never any question about you having the wedding here."

Tears of gratitude blurred Kate's vision. "Thank you, Hannah. You have been a very true friend. I don't know what I'd have done without you."

If her uncle Brandon had offered her and Sarah a home, Kate would have hated leaving Hannah's friendship behind.

Her friend looked over from putting a stack of cups in the cabinets. Beaming, she said, "What are friends for, Kate, if not to help one another. I know you'd help me, if ever I need you. It's as God wishes."

"Of all my friends here, you have been the best." Kate only briefly thought of sharing her conflicts with Hannah, dismissing it again. Her friend was very happy in her life and she wouldn't have been able to understand Kate's questions.

"Nonsense. Someone else would have stepped up if I hadn't been able to." Hannah lowered her voice, "John and I will bed the children down in their room, as usual, and then we'll make a pallet in here for you and Enoch. I know you'll be staying here to help us finish the clean-up tomorrow."

Her friend's words sent Kate's thoughts into overdrive again. When they were courting years ago, the thought of lying down next to Enoch in the dark had brought a mixture of excitement and nerves, but now? Now, things were even more complicated than she could have ever imagined. The image of lying in bed with him now brought very different fears. Enoch had married her and promised to care for her and Sarah—even knowing how she secretly felt. Even though they'd courted before and she'd rejected his decree.

With so much water under the bridge, could he ever truly forgive her?

"—and Sarah can sleep in the other bedroom with the older children," Hannah went on. "She won't mind for just one night."

"Are you kidding?" Kate cleared her throat to fake a chuckle as her daughter raced past with Hannah's eldest. "She'll be thrilled."

An hour later, the darkened house even more quiet as the children retired to their beds, John helped Enoch spread quilts in a pile. "I think this will be comfortable enough."

He tugged at the corner of the top quilt.

"Kate and I will be fine here," Enoch assured him. "Thank you."

"No problem, my brother." John's smile was silly. "Now that you've married my Hannah's best friend, I think I can call you that."

"Of course." Enoch wasn't sure what else to say, but the Hochstetlers had been very generous.

"Do you think this will be enough quilts?"

"Yes." Enoch patted the pallet he was to share with Kate. "Very comfortable."

"Good, good." John turned toward the kitchen area, lifting a plain candle holder. "Well, Hannah, I'm sure you need to rest. Come lie down and put your feet up."

In a very short time, their hosts had said goodnight, Kate disappeared into the bathroom, taking a candle with her.

Enoch sat on the pallet brooding into the shadows. He'd prayed and prayed about this and he believed—for whatever reasons—God had led him into this marriage. Even with the tangle of feelings he felt for the woman soon to lie down next to him.

No one had ever made him as angry as Kate—and no one had ever inspired him with such compassion and hunger. He didn't know whether to kiss her or strangle her. Being married now didn't change that.

She would soon lie next to him as his wife and the thought made Enoch both exultant and cautious. He realized that he now had her where he'd wanted her. She'd come to him, asking for rescue and he'd taken in her and the child in the only way he could.

His was now the power. She needed him...since her beloved Uncle Brandon hadn't come through... Soon they would lie together, build a life together and, God-willing, bring forth children. Only Enoch sat there in the gloom waiting for Kate and knew he wanted more. He didn't want just a willing wife, a woman who tolerated his presence in the house. He wanted Kate to want to be his wife. Even though just the thought of her rejection of him for Jakob Bieler still bit into his soul no matter how he tried to pray it away.

When she came back into the living room, Enoch was stretched out on his side of the pallet, the covers pulled to his waist, his hands behind his head. A single candle burned on the closest small table.

Glancing over, he saw that she wore a voluminous flowered nightgown, a blanket shawl around her shoulders. The room was very quiet, the giggles from the children's room faded away.

Kate cast a nervous glance his way and Enoch saw the worry behind her blue eyes—even in the shadows. It wasn't what he wanted. He didn't want Kate to be afraid of him, even though some part of him was angry at her.

"It's warmer in here," he said, pulling her side of the blanket back. In that moment, he could have kicked himself at the silliness of his words. Of course it was warm under the covers.

"Fine. Good. I'll be right there."

The words and the tone in which she uttered them conveyed her anxiety at being with him, even though he thought he'd been clear about what the marriage would involve. And he wasn't her first. Enoch realized that wasn't what disturbed him, but that she'd turned to another man. She'd angrily pushed aside all he'd said, gone defiantly off to Baltimore and come back just as defiant from her *rumpringa* time, only to marry another man.

In the months and years since they had courted, he'd remembered often the smooth softness of Kate's mouth in their chaste kisses, the clean, sweet smell of her. Enoch swallowed.

Beside the pallet, her back now to him, Kate fussed with taking off her slippers, setting her candle on the table and blowing them both out.

Darkness suddenly enveloped the room and for that moment, Enoch felt no anger towards her. He could feel her in the blankets next to him. Fussing with her long nightgown, tugging the covers over her as she lie on her back. He could feel the nervousness radiating from her.

He looked up into the darkness, grabbing for his ragged sanity. She smelled good, lying there beside him.

"Calm yourself." The words came out of him before he realized it, his voice low.

"What?" There was a faint squeak to her response.

"Calm yourself, Kate. We'll deal with everything tomorrow…when we're home. It'll all sort out." The words just came to him and Enoch knew he meant them. "Don't worry yourself."

Reaching over, he patted her through the covers. "Just rest. It's been a long day. Tomorrow we'll get home and settle you and Sarah in."

She'd gone still beneath his pat and she said nothing for a moment. Then she said in a quiet, almost-timid voice that wasn't like the Kate he'd known from former days. "Thank you, Enoch. I-I'm sure we will…work it all out."

He grimaced into the darkness, rolled over in their pallet and pulled the quilt up over his shoulder, not sure how he could feel at peace with what he'd done and still be so angry with Kate. Somehow he had to stop thinking of her lying next to Jakob like this.

CHAPTER FOUR

"I'm not sure what you're upset about, Kate." A week later, Hannah sat at the table in Enoch's warm kitchen across from Kate, a cup of tea cradled in her hands, blonde corkscrews springing free from beneath her *kapp*. "From what you've said your husband has been thoughtful and considerate."

"It's just that Enoch treats me like nothing more than a random community member at worship services," Kate said to her teacup, staring into the dark brew. "We sleep in the same bed at night, but always stay on our own sides. It's almost as if we're bundling, not fully married."

She fell silent, suddenly awash in memories of her courting time with Enoch. Tall and powerfully built with dark, dark eyes and skin that ripened in the sun. He was so strong and he made her laugh... Kissed her like he couldn't get enough of her. What had happened?

From the nearby hearth, the crackle of logs burning could be heard and the room was filled with the pleasant smell.

"But what do you expect?" Hannah looked at her across the sturdy kitchen work table, her pale eyebrows raised. "There was all the business of the wedding sermon—you know we served two hundred people that day, maybe more. And then you two bedded down on a pallet in our living room—you didn't even have a private room to yourself—after which you spent the whole next day helping us get the house back in order."

"And when we finally came back to this home?" Kate couldn't help the frustration in her chest, the pale teacup warm, smooth between her hands. "I'm just worried that Enoch is…still angry with me. For what happened in the past."

"If that was true," Hannah said practically, "why marry you? Besides, Sarah is here with you. It's not every young couple that has a child in their home from the first of their marriage. That can be distracting. No wonder you and Enoch are getting a slow start."

Kate's teacup settled on the table top with a clatter. She looked significantly at her friend's swollen belly. "Well, that certainly hasn't stopped you and John. This will be your fifth…and baby Lydia has slept in your bedroom."

Hannah laughed. "Not anymore, I remind you. John finished her bed and we shifted her into the other room with her brothers and sister two nights ago."

Not able to help the cluster of anxiety that crawled up her neck from her chest, Kate said, "Enoch's house has not three, but four bedrooms. Big ones, too, and Sarah's room is down the hall. Further than your children sleep from you and John."

She shook her head. "I haven't told you all of it, but when we parted years back—after courting for nearly six months—Enoch and I had a really big fight."

"I knew he didn't want you to visit with your Uncle Brandon for your *rumspringa* for some reason. That's all you said." Hannah's voice was placid. "Although you never really went into why he felt that way."

Under the flood of memories of that time, Kate bent her head, the strings of her starched *kapp* brushing her chest. "It wasn't just that. He told me that I shouldn't—that girls didn't need a *rumspringa*, at all. Oh, he got all ridiculous about women in our church, saying all kinds of things. About how girls have it so much easier than men and that there was no reason for me to go to Baltimore. He was bossy and mean. I was furious with him."

"But it was years ago. Have you spoken to him about any of this?" Her friend ventured to ask with lifted brows. "The past…and now?"

Kate looked up at her friend. "And what would I have said? That he was unfair all those years ago and why doesn't he want to—to do more than sleep with me now that we're married? I can't say those things."

"I'm not sure you have anything to worry about. This can't continue. Every man wants a family. Bopplis of his own? It is God's way and God's gift. Enoch has been alone too long."

Staring down at the now-tepid brown liquid in her cup, Kate said in words that came slowly, "He was very, very angry with me when I went to Baltimore."

Lifting her head, she met her friend's blue gaze. "What if he's still angry and he can never forgive me? Maybe he married me as a sort of revenge. Married, but not really."

Hannah laughed. "Sweetie, don't be so dramatic. If Enoch wanted revenge, you and Sarah were in a pretty bad spot before he married you. He could have refused your proposal and watched you struggle. You didn't know what to do."

Had it only been five years back that she'd known she would be by his side as long as she lived? And then he'd been unfair, so angry and so insistent that she had no need to go on *rumspringa*. Only to her parents and Enoch had she talked of her simmering doubts about the restrictions of their faith.

She loved her simple, plain life, but she'd been raised by a post-feminism mother who was a rare convert to their religion and to an Amish life. She had questions about how the Ordnung dealt with women's role in the church and in the family. College-educated Elizabeth Lehman had taught Kate after she'd finished the eighth grade of schooling considered in their church as all a child needed. Elizabeth had loved her life here and never felt the need to venture back into the *Englisch* world, but she'd never scolded Kate for having questions.

But she and James Lehman had listened to Kate's frustrations and doubts. Her mother had agreed that she had some points in her issues. She hated that women had no role in the church and—though often the family financial stewards—were viewed as wives and mothers, but nothing more.

It was her observation that both men and women could be foolish in this world and that God loved both sexes, even though they neither deserved it. How did men get elevated somehow? She'd never understood.

Elizabeth had been honest, telling her both the good and bad of the *Englisch* life. Her parents had never said that she should make the same choices they'd made. But Enoch had gone silent when she shared her thoughts on the restriction of women in the Amish world. When he did talk—actually forbidding her to go on *rumspringa*—he'd told her she had no business questioning the roles of women in their Amish world. Or questioning any part of their Ordnung-defined lives.

Getting up from the table to carry her used white teacup to the sink, Hannah stopped beside where she sat, patting her hand. "It will all work out, Kate. You will see. You and Enoch will be fine and you'll be growing a baby in no time."

Watching her walk away toward the sink, Kate wondered how she and Enoch could ever breach this gulf.

"I'm telling you, Isaac," Enoch said, the handle of the fork smooth in his hands as the brothers pitched fresh hay out for Enoch's cows, "the woman is a pitiful cook. It's a wonder little Sarah has survived. My stomach has been grumbling all week."

"Cooking is complicated. Not all women know how to do it well right away."

Isaac chuckled. "Maybe Jakob's accident happened because he was starved and not paying attention to his work."

A shaft of anger went through him and Enoch sucked in a breath of the sweet hay dusk, knowing he had to get over feeling jealous of a dead man. "*Ya.* That might have been it."

The younger man suggested, "Maybe you could get Mother to come give her lessons."

"I probably should." Enoch continued thrusting the pitchfork tines into the clump of hay near the barn, registering the clean, dusty scent.

"I think she's mad at me."

Isaac stopped in his work, staring at his brother. "Why should she be?"

He didn't want to answer his brother's question, not liking to remember all he'd said to her in their big fight years ago. Shrugging, Enoch merely said, "Kate just seems mad. She does her work, of course—making her pitiful food for us all, feeding the chickens, getting the cows milked. You know, all that. But she seems—I don't know—annoyed."

Leaning to shove the scoop into the feed bin, Isaac recommended, "I think you shouldn't draw any conclusions, brother. She probably knows she's not a good cook and she's worried, that's all."

Enoch said nothing, putting feed out for larger animals.

He'd always known he wanted to farm the land, even as a kinder, not feeling in any hurry to start courting any girl, but Kate Lehman had blossomed in ways he couldn't ignore. Before he knew it, he was seeking her out at the Sunday night sings and sneaking off to canoodle with her behind her father's barn, the crickets' chirping in the woods around them as he'd learned how much fun kissing could be.

Remembering the time as if it had happened the day before, Enoch moved to start cleaning out the horses' stalls while Isaac stacked hay.

"I appreciate your help, Brother. I'm sure Dad has things that need doing."

Isaac shrugged. "I'll get to those things, too. Right now, Brother, I just wanted to make sure how you and Kate are getting along. I probably shouldn't stay for dinner, though."

"No," Enoch laughed as he looked over at his younger brother, "you shouldn't."

Even though he wasn't looking forward to the meal a few nights later, Enoch was happy their neighbors came to join them.

"I'm so glad you invited John and I and the children to eat with you," Hannah said affectionately as the men and children sat at the long dining table. She and Kate moved between the table and the kitchen, serving out the food.

The hum of chattering voices filled the spacious room and Enoch smiled. At the other end of the table, the oldest Hochstetler girl in her dark dress and a little white prayer *kapp* that matched her mother's sat alongside her brothers in their dark pants and white shirts. As Hannah moved to help Kate dish out the stew, she balanced a baby on her hip, moving more gracefully than a very pregnant woman should be able to.

Leaning back as Kate reached around him to put a full bowl in his place, he tried not to look too depressed.

Enoch glanced at the kids as she dished stew into their bowls, bent over at their places, as if inhaling the scent of the meal—and he felt a pang he couldn't fully decipher. They were all such good little *Boppli*, sitting carefully at the table with little Sarah.

He just hoped Kate's food didn't choke them. It smelled good enough and he was grateful that she'd managed not to burn it like she had the food for their last two suppers.

Next to him, Hannah's husband, John, arranged his napkin over his chest, as if preparing to chow down like the hungry sows in the pen outside.

The women continued passing out hearty-looking rolls that were probably as heavy as dirt clods.

Lowering his voice only a little—as Kate and Hannah were busy getting the food on the table—Enoch bent toward John to say, "Don't be too hard on Kate. She's just learning to cook and the stew will be pitiful. I just hope none of you break a tooth on her rolls. I'm sure you normally eat better. It's a wonder Sarah's not skin and bones if she's been eating Kate's food these past four years. I've been meaning to see if my mother will come give her lessons."

He manfully hoisted a spoonful of stew to his lips, careful to school his features to reveal nothing. As he took a swallow, a hefty amount of salt landed on his taste buds.

John looked over with a startled express. "What do you mean? Kate's a great cook. Why she's made some of the best meals we've had. Even taught my Hannah a thing or two."

Glancing up to meet his guest's astonished face, Enoch frowned as he said slowly. "What are you saying?"

"Only that Kate cooks wonderful food." The other man looked at him as if he were nuts. "Why I've told Hannah that no other woman is ever to be allowed to help out when we have sermons at our house—or when she's in bed from having a *Boppli*. Kate's a wonder at the stove. It's a gift. The meals she's made for us would bring tears to your eyes."

John started laughing. "She must have started cooking with her mother when she was my Abigail's age. You know the Lehman's had no other *Boppli*. I'm sure Elizabeth had lots of time to cook with Kate."

Hearing John Hochstetler singing Kate's praises, Enoch felt himself turning to stone, his mind flashing back to the miserable meals he endured in the last week. He'd been thinking of taking a hand at it himself, just until she got adjusted.

But she was a good cook? When she wasn't cooking for him? Anger that had been simmering, jumped into his chest.

He was a fool! Slowly, he replayed their first week together. Actually, the first day or so after returning from their wedding at the Hochstetler home, Kate had made meals that were pretty good, considering how horrible the rest of it had been.

And little Sarah had said nothing at those sad mealtimes later in the week. He'd absently registered that she'd gotten snacks from Kate and, other than thinking the child had a cast-iron stomach that was no doubt accustomed to abuse, he hadn't even wondered at it.

Realizing that the kitchen had grown quiet other than the sound of John still chuckling, Enoch wrestled with his surging anger.

"Kate came to feed us all when Hannah had Lydia." John Hochstetler spooned stew into his mouth and then stopped, looking down at his bowl in surprise. "Why this is wonderful, Enoch."

Staring down the table at the woman he'd married, Enoch said in a hard voice, "Give me a taste from your bowl, John."

At the sound of his words, Kate turned to meet his eyes as he dipped his spoon in the bowl John held out in confusion, a hint of laughter in her gaze.

Enoch lifted a spoonful of stew from his neighbor's bowl, keeping his gaze locked with hers. Flavors burst on his tongue, warm and tasty, as he confirmed that she'd been making a fool of him.

John was right. She was a good cook, going by the stew in his neighbor's bowl.

"You know, Hannah, I've always thought," his new wife smirked at him as she continued ladling stew into the children's bowls, "that a woman's cooking reflects how she feels."

For the first time ever, Enoch could see how a husband might want to beat his wife—not that he would—but he wanted to.

"Yes, I believe that's true." Oblivious to her hosts' byplay, Hannah continued serving out rolls.

Enoch glared at Kate, knowing that the man who sat beside him had grown quiet and was staring at them.

"Of course," Kate's fake smile widened as she turned to serve out stew to another child, "I've also heard it said that the way to a man's heart is through his stomach."

Just as Hannah looked up to flash a glance between Enoch and Kate—apparently noting finally the change in her friend's voice— little Sarah spoke up from her spot near the end of the table. "Poor Papa Enoch's stomach has been hurting all week. He had to take bicarbonate of soda, it got so bad."

His anger ratcheting up, he felt himself suffuse with hot fury, Enoch heard Hannah's soft laughter at his step-daughter's remark.

Here he'd done the woman who jilted him a huge favor and she'd repaid him by turning him into a laughingstock for his neighbors. The woman deserved to be thrashed.

Later that evening when the Hochstetlers had left and Sarah finally gone to bed, Kate washed the remaining dishes from the evening meal, her hands thrust into the warm sudsy dish water. She was acutely aware that she was now alone with a very angry Enoch. Out of the corner of her eye, she saw him standing at the end of the kitchen counter after he'd closed the door behind the last of their guests.

"I guess you enjoyed making me look like a fool."

Reacting as much to the harshness in his tone as to his words, Kate spun around to face him. Hot words spilled out of her, "Well, aren't you doing the same to me? Making a fool of me?"

They stood in the kitchen, his hands bracketed at his waist; hers held in front of her, damp and soapy from the dish water. She tried to keep her angry hissing tones low, so as not to disturb Sarah who she hoped was asleep upstairs. She and Enoch glared at one another and it was as if time fell away. Again they faced one another in anger. They were young and in love years ago and so much at odds—over what all she couldn't say, but she remembered the scent of him…and the power in his embrace. Everything was all so wrong.

"In front of my neighbors, Kate? There I was worried about your feelings getting hurt about your terrible cooking and I ended up looking like an idiot!" He matched her low voice, the tone vibrating with anger. "A fool! You are apparently renown for your cooking—something I've yet to see—because you are deliberately making awful food, just for me!"

"And we all know that women aren't allowed to make decisions! We just cook."

"Decisions?"

"No." Her voice was low and angry. "We make food and don't have any part in how things go in a marriage."

"I have no idea what you're talking about." His voice was exasperated and he ran a frustrated hand over his forehead, raking his fingers through his hair.

Pushing aside her lingering feeling of guilt at having set him up so, Kate spat back in lowered words. "Tell me this! Why do you have all the power in our marriage, Enoch? Why are you the only one who gets to make all the decisions?"

Feeling angry tears threatening to spill down her cheeks, she whipped back to the sink, bracing her hands there against the countertop until the corner bit into her flesh.

"What are you talking about?" He still sounded exasperated. "I have no idea what you mean. We've only been married a week. I don't see that I've made any decisions with or without you."

To her shame salty moisture leaked from her eyes. Kate wanted to sniffle back the tears, but she knew the sound would give her away. She kept her back to him. "Why did you even marry me if you're so angry at me still? Why put me and Sarah through this?"

This was where her mother would have cautioned her to think before she spoke, but Kate couldn't hold her feelings back.

"Now, wait a minute, woman." He sounded like he'd come closer. "You and that little girl were in big trouble. You'd have had no other choice, except to marry that *Boppli*, Aaron Yoder, or bed down with John and Hannah's children, if I hadn't—"

No longer worried about him seeing her tears, Kate whirled around to face him. "What? If you hadn't taken us in? Out of some Godly act of kindness? Do you even want to be my husband, Enoch?"

She turned back to the sink, blindly lifting the pan to dump out the dishwater. As it splashed against the sides of the sink before running down the drain, she felt a tear trickle down her cheek.

After the beat of several seconds, Enoch asked in a kinder tone, "What is this all about, Katie? Do you still hate me?"

Kate drew in a shuddering breath, drying her damp hands on a nearby towel before she slowly turned.

Enoch—tall and broad, his suspenders hanging on the shoulders she'd clung to when he kissed her as a *youngie*—stood facing her, his expression troubled. "Do you, Kate? Do you still hate me? Like when you had nothing to do with me after spending time in Baltimore? And then you up and married Jakob Bieler? I never even knew why you were so angry. I mean, other than our big fight over you running off to your uncle."

Rolling her head back to stare up at the kitchen ceiling before straightening to look at him, Kate sniffled back her remaining tears, saying, "I never hated you, Enoch. It was you hating me all those years ago. Hating that I had a backbone, that I had thoughts of my own. At least, Jakob said he liked that about me."

"Don't be ridiculous." He looked at her with narrowed eyes, his voice hardening. "I liked that you had—have—thoughts of your own. It was just that, as a girl, you had things to learn. There's no shame in that."

"You didn't like that I thought women should be allowed a place in the church—that I thought *rumspringa* was for both boys and girls. I still think those things, Enoch. My going to Baltimore and—and marrying Jakob didn't change that." Some of the heat had drained out of her words and she looked at him with a pierced heart.

Enoch waved a hand between them. "We've gotten off course here, Katie. We're talking about you making a fool of me by pretending you couldn't cook."

Pausing to dry her hands further on a dishtowel, she then set it aside. "No, Enoch. This is about much more than cooking."

"Well, why don't you tell me what it's about?" His words were frustrated and he sounded anything, but encouraging. "Cause I was the one who looked like a fool tonight."

Without even thinking, she asked the question that had returned to her again and again. "All those years ago, Enoch...why didn't you write me in Baltimore? Or answer the letter I sent to you?"

He said nothing, just standing there in the kitchen, stocky and muscular in his plain white shirt, his face wearing that unreadable expression she hated.

"Why did you marry me?" She carefully leached the hurt out of her question. "It doesn't seem that you want me as a husband wants a wife."

Enoch still said nothing, them both facing one another. Only three feet away, she felt as if the gulf between them was miles wide.

After a moment, his words came low. "You needed a place to live, you and Sarah. Isn't that why you married me? Isn't this a practical arrangement?"

She put up her hands to rub at her eyes, pressing then against her hot cheeks. Nothing was simple between them. Maybe she should have married young Aaron Yoder. "I think you're trying to punish me for—for going to Uncle Brandon's on my *rumspringa*. For marrying someone else when I returned…instead of drying up and blowing away from the misery between us."

Enoch took a step toward her, his face dark with anger and other feelings she couldn't decipher. In a furious undertone, he said, "I married you, Kate Miller, and I certainly plan to be your husband. In every way. You committed to me—to work beside me, to bear my kinder. To be my wife. I've held back—lying beside you every night, surrounded by the scent of you—because I wanted to give you time to adjust. Because…you're still in mourning for your parents. Because I've been trying to do the right thing! But you can count on that stopping right now. You've made a mock of me for my thoughtfulness and it is clearly time I stopped worrying about your feelings."

His words came out hard and fast, matching the glitter in his eyes.

Her jaw dropped in astonishment, Kate's breath was suspended in her chest. Responding to the anger she saw in his face, finally not expressionless, she swallowed. Frustration and wrath rolled off him, the waves of it shaking her. She had the urge to falter back a step, but felt glued to the floor. This intense, mad Enoch was…like the boy she'd falling in love with. And not. He was scary.

At the same time, his words seemed to clear up her fears that he no longer wanted her as a wife.

CHAPTER FIVE

A week later, his work finished for the afternoon, Enoch felt the cool fall air wash over him as he walked down the rough buggy drive to where his post box was planted next to the lane that wound by his farm. The pastures on either side of the path were lined with rows of the dry brown stalks of harvested feed corn. A rain storm had blown through the previous evening and he could smell the dampness of the dirt, even though the sun shone warm on his shoulders.

Reaching up to his chin, he scratched at the itchy beard growing in now that he was married. Soon he'd look like the mated-man he was now.

A few puddles still lingered on either side of the drive, but he heard the whispering of insects out and about. Occasionally, moths fluttered along the breeze, landing on a taller corn stalk. It was a peaceful moment and he reflected again that this life fit him like a glove. He loved it.

Autumn was a lighter time of year, but as he strode down the lane Enoch felt the work of the day in his body, a stretch of muscles well-used.

There was no denying the spring in his step, even after hours of labor. Despite his hesitance to follow a path of what veered close to vengeance, his marriage to Kate had definite benefits.

John Hostetler was right.

She could cook like an angel…when she wasn't trying to starve him. And having her in his bed as his wife wasn't too bad either now that she'd removed any over-concern he'd had about her feeling awkward in their marriage.

His mind wandering as he went down the drying lane, Enoch thought of her face as she'd asked him why he hadn't written when she was off on *rumspringa*, the strain in her blue eyes. He remembered having gotten her letter from Baltimore, of reading it and wondering what all she'd left out. He'd fallen hard for Kate, seeing her blossom from a tall, weedy *youngie* into a beautiful, beautiful woman.

It had killed him to think she might let another man kiss her when out in the *Englisch* world, might allow other men privileges he'd thought of as his own even then. Kate had been his woman. He'd struggled with how to keep her safe by his side. And then she'd been stubborn, going off on *rumspringa*, no matter how he tried to stop her.

The ping of a yellow grasshopper shooting out of the field next to him jerked Enoch from his memories. Much had passed since those days and now here he was married to Kate.

Their battle after the Hochstetler family left had cleared the air somewhat and set them on a better path. Now that Kate was his wife in every meaning of the word, they'd settled into a routine that was sometimes comfortable, sometimes heart-pounding. He'd never expected her to be so…so loving in that part of their lives. Certainly not after their heated interchange in the kitchen after the Hochstetlers left.

To his relief, though, their fight had seemed to bring Kate and him closer.

Just having her sleep next to him—the warmth of her soft body seeping into his—made every day brighter. He'd noticed that the first night of her being there and every night since and it was better now. Even before they'd hollered at one another in the kitchen and come to this new understanding, having her sleeping beside him just felt right. She was his wife now. His wife.

To his left, a flock of crows circled, yelling at one another as they drifted down to land on the fallow field.

Enoch continued to the postal box, his forehead wrinkling a little under his broad-brimmed straw hat. He didn't know what to make of the woman and that was unsettling, too. He knew she sometimes felt chafed at the ways of their lives. But she mothered little Sarah wonderfully, kept them all in clean clothes and worked to weed the expansive garden beside the house. All as a woman of God should do.

Hannah Hostetler had even made mention at supper that Hannah had only helped a little with the simple purple bridal dress Kate wore to their marriage. Most of the stitching work had been Kate's and he'd seen the quilt she worked on in the evenings, beautiful in its simplicity.

He had a hard time matching all that up with the questions she'd admitted to when she'd confided in him as a youngie and had restated in their low-voiced argument just days ago. She still had rebellious thoughts clearly, but those didn't keep her from fulfilling her tasks.

Was this just a measure of having grown up? Or had her marriage to Jakob somehow changed her? For some reason, the possibility left his stomach feeling sick inside him. But he knew she wasn't completely settled in her thoughts. She'd even admitted that she'd written to her *Englischer* uncle for help after her parents died. How could a woman so apparently happy with the life think of leaving it?

Just then something slithered through the grass alongside the buggy path and Enoch stopped in respect. The snake wasn't close to the house and if it was a rat snake, it had a function.

Continuing on in a minute or so, Enoch stopped beside the post box and riffled briefly through the mail there. He stopped when his hand came to an envelope that had "Forward" stamped across it and a typed address. It was sent to Kate Bieler.

He recognized the address as the house Kate's father had rented. This had to have been sent before her marriage was known. His gaze zipping to the return address, Enoch's grip on the envelope tightened.

Baltimore. Kate's Uncle Brandon had finally responded.

A string of thoughts streaked through Enoch's mind. It was to her uncle's house that she'd gone for *rumspringa* years back, by the very act telling Enoch she wouldn't let him direct her behavior. And when she proposed to him now, she'd told Enoch that her uncle hadn't replied to her letter, an unspoken implication that if her uncle had opened the door, she'd have gone there with little Sarah.

Instead of marrying Enoch.

Without further hesitation, he ripped open the envelope and jerked the letter from inside it.

Kate was now his wife. He had the right to open her mail. Particularly this letter.

Crumpling the envelope in his left hand, he stood in the lane, frowning at the typed paper clutched so tightly in his hand that the paper wrinkled some.

"...been out of town on work...deep sadness at the news of my sister's death. ...of course you and your daughter are welcome here."

Enoch stared down at the letter, the words blurring a little beneath his gaze.

There it was, then. Kate did have another option. Another place to go now that her father's rented house had been claimed by its owner. Another option besides being married to Enoch. Even though they were joined in front of God.

Staring across his field, Enoch was barely aware of the breeze having kicked up and grown sharper. Chilled air skittered across the back of his shirt, but he only walked away from the mail box to brace himself against the rough rail fence that circled his land, staring still at the paper in his hand.

Kate's possible reaction to the letter played across his thoughts. With her uncle's response, she could retreat to Baltimore, if she chose. Even though they were married now in the eyes of God. She'd proposed and he'd accepted, housing her and little Sarah.

And since she was now his wife in all ways, she could even carry his child with her.

How could he let that happen? He couldn't let her leave now. Enoch wrestled with himself. Surely God wouldn't have given him a warm wife—so ready to be his in all ways that she got angry when he didn't lie with her—and have him lose her? God wouldn't want that.

Slowly, Enoch let himself acknowledge what he was considering. He didn't have to mention this letter. To anyone. Not to Isaac or his parents. Not to Kate.

She didn't need to know anything about it.

They had come together and committed to one another before the Lord and the community. There was no divorce in their world, no matter what the *Englischers* chose to do. They were married for life. Husband and wife.

Who would benefit if she got this letter? Kate seemed very content with her lot. She hadn't even talked much of her dissatisfaction with church elders. Every action now seemed directed toward building a home with Enoch and Sarah. Settling in here…to have his Boppli and sleep every night beside him.

He'd been hesitant to marry her with such dark hurt in his heart, but it had worked out. Hadn't it?

With fingers made clumsy by the struggle within him, Enoch slowly folded the paper and stuffed it in his shirt.

An autumn breeze skittering around her skirts, Kate stepped around the hen house to scatter grain to feed the chickens. Off in the distance, she could hear Enoch clanging around behind the barn.

The hens had provided well this morning. As she mused over dinner possibilities, Sarah stuck her head around the gate. "I've finished my chores, *Mamm*. Can I read now?"

The child's interest in the written word was great and startling, given that her father hadn't been much of a reader.

"Yes, child. Will you be in your room?"

Blonde plaits on either side of her face wiggling as she shook her head, Sarah smiled. "I think I'll read in the barn. The cows like me reading to them as they eat."

Chuckling, Kate nodded. "Fine. Suit yourself. I'll call you in for supper."

Outside the far side of the barn, Enoch tried to ignore the rustling feel of the letter from Kate's uncle that he'd thrust into his shirt at the post box an hour before. Cleaning the equipment he used to till the fields, he lowered his head and tried to banish the angry thoughts crowding in.

Autumn—when all the harvests were in—was the best time to remove any dirt and rust and sharpen the blades that would cut into the earth next spring and the work kept him busy. Soon it would be time to help his mom bring the fall harvest from her garden to sell at the roadside stand. If all had gone the way he'd planned, his wife would add vegetables from her garden to the stand next fall. Now, he just wondered if she'd still be there with him.

Although his hands stayed busy with these tasks, he was acutely aware that Kate worked in the house on the other side of the barn, maybe cleaning the kitchen's planed wooden floors or getting food cooking for their supper meal. Probably wondering why her uncle hadn't responded to her letter…

Although the sun was starting its afternoon descent down toward the earth, nothing was quiet, the scratch of his metal brush against the equipment mingling with the whirring sound of cicadas joined with the whisper-crackle of other insects. It was almost as if he could hear the swelling, falling background noise when he put the wire brush down.

Enoch scrubbed the brush hard against the metal farm equipment, his thoughts circling.

Kate not only maintained her connection to the *Englischer* world all these years, she'd tried to move into it after her parents died, preferring to seek assistance from her non-Amish uncle rather than from her own people.

He couldn't imagine not living this plain, simple life. It held all the really important basics—God, family and friends he'd known his whole life. Fresh air and hard, clean work in the fields where he raised his own crops and cared for the farm animals.

Still scrubbing at a stubborn clump of hardened dirt, Enoch became aware of a child's voice in the barn. It sounded as if Sarah were reciting or giving the cows and chickens a lecture. He could see a solemn child like her doing this. The thought made his lips twist in a half-smile. He'd gotten better at not mentally inserting Jakob Bieler's child into every Sarah-thought, but Enoch knew he hadn't yet completely warmed up to the young girl. It wasn't her fault, though, that her father had married Enoch's woman.

After listening a moment to her childish voice, he deliberately put down the wire brush and stepped into the barn, telling himself he'd get a swallow of water from the rain barrel that sat outside the other side of the barn. The familiar smell of animals and hay immediately surrounded him.

There on a small wooden milking stool beside a line of cows that munched stoically from their feed troughs as dust motes floated through the air was young Sarah, the gray folds of her skirt falling around her sturdy shoes, a book open on her lap. She was reading aloud.

Enoch pushed a half-smile onto his face as he stepped into the dusty, dim light inside the barn, knowing he had to stop scowling at the child although his heart felt black with anger and, deeper down, a disappointment he didn't want to acknowledge.

None of this was her fault, though.

Bent over the book, Sarah read aloud, "...if you see something resembling a shark in a river, don't fret. It's more likely to be a small submarine operated by thieves."

The words she read took a moment to sink into his brain. What was this nonsense the child was looking at?

Stepping further into the barn, he said, "What are you reading, child?"

Sarah looked up, her hazel-brown eyes cautious. "I...I'm reading my book to the cows."

Noting the cautiousness in her voice, Enoch frowned as he walked over to where Sarah sat. He held out his hand for the book and looked down at the worn paperback, the letter to Kate crackling against his skin as he moved. The faded, surprisingly-lurid book cover showed a young *Englisch* girl shining a light up a dark, ominous stone staircase. "Where did you get it?"

Handing the book to him slowly, she said in a nervous voice that held a shade of defiance, "*Mamm* gave it to me. She knows I'm here. I finished my chores and she said I might read a little."

"Kate gave you this book?" He couldn't help the way his words rapped out.

The child's chin went up in a way that was vaguely reminiscent of the mother who hadn't borne her. "Yes, she did."

Sarah shifted on her stool. "She said it belonged to her mother once."

"Naturally." The word tasted bitter in his mouth. "Well, never mind. I'll take it into the house now. Check to see that the hens have been fed."

"Yes, sir." The girl jumped up from the stool where he loomed over her, scuttling out of the barn.

Stalking out of the barn, Enoch went across the faded green of the yard, mounting the wooden steps as he told himself to settle down, to not speak hasty words he'd regret. Some might say his reaction to Sarah's reading material was heightened by how tangled thing with Kate were. Even that it had something to do with his decision to keep the letter to himself. It didn't matter. Letting her read that *Englischer* book wasn't right.

The minute he passed through the doorway the mouth-watering smell of newly baked bread enveloped him. Seeing Kate bent to close the oven door, everything inside him bubbled up.

"What is this, Kate?"

Clearly startled by his entrance into the kitchen—and by what even he recognized as the harsh tone of his words—Kate swung round when he started speaking.

He held the book up. "You gave this to Sarah? An *Englischer* book about thieves? Why give her this? Are you trying to poison her against our life? You know God would not like this."

"A book about thieves?" She clutched at her apron as if to dry damp hands. "I don't know what you're talking about."

"Your daughter." He still held the book up to show the faded cover, shaking it a little. "You gave her this to read."

Coming toward him, Kate took the book. "What? Oh, a Nancy Drew mystery. It was my mother's."

"And you believe this is fit reading for Sarah? No wonder you grew up with so many questions and doubts, if your mother gave you *Englischer* books like this to read."

Kate gasped, her voice rising in pitch as she asked, "Are you blaming my mother? For—for the questions I admitted to? Let me remind you that my wonderful mother was born in the *Englisch* world! She fell in love with my father and decided of her own free will to leave that world to embrace his lifestyle and his beliefs!"

The thought streaked across his brain that Kate obviously didn't love him in that way, like her mother had her father. If Kate cared for him, at all....

"I am not trying to be subversive with Sarah." She brushed angrily at her eyes. "Nancy Drew mysteries aren't harmful. The heroine outwits the thieves and bad guys."

"I'm not even sure what subversive means, but you think this book is the best reading for an eight year-old girl? How can she even make sense of it? She doesn't know this life."

Kate brushed her hands again uneasily over her apron. "Well, she might not make sense of all of it, but Sarah's a great reader. She's years ahead of the other children her age and I thought it would be good for her to try a more complicated book. Nancy Drew books are classic reading for children."

Watching her stammering words come to a halt, Enoch asked, trying to keep the bitterness out of his voice, "And you think this will prepare Sarah for our plain, simple life? That it's better for her to read this garbage than be out playing in the sunshine?"

"It can't hurt her." Kate's hands settled on her hips. "There is nothing specifically un-Godly in that book."

"Just from the cover, I'd doubt that. Would the elders approve of it? I don't think so. The child should be reading her Bible, if she wants to read."

"Enoch," she paused, seeming to bite back hot words, "I've raised this child since she was five years-old. There is no way to keep her from reading, even if I wanted to. She does her chores. Except for her occasional stubbornness, Sarah's a good child. Why not let her read an interesting book?"

It went all over him that she'd even been in the marriage with Jakob to be a step-mother to the girl for three years.

"It isn't right," Enoch insisted. "You must make her stop. Let her help you more in the garden if she needs occupation."

"Sarah does help me. We've already cleaned a patch to the side of the house."

"I'm sure there is more to do."

She stood in front of him, looking at him with angry blue eyes, her back to the stove, the clean scent of her soap mingling with the smell of fresh-baked bread.

Bitterness rolled in his stomach as Enoch reminded himself that she'd only married him because her uncle's letter had been delayed.

"There is always more to do, Enoch." Kate's chest rose with her agitated breathing. "But let me ask you something—do you ever intend to become Sarah's father? You brought us into this house—marrying me after promising to shelter and love me in God's eyes. Didn't that include my child?"

"Sarah is not your child." He regretted the words as soon as they were out of his mouth.

Kate took an impulsive step forward, the scrubbed table between them. "Yes, she is! She's my child, Enoch. As if I'd borne her in my own body. Mine. I love her, watch over her, enjoy her. She's mine. We are a package—Sarah and me. I thought you knew that."

He felt rooted to the floor, the woman in front of him flushed from the heat of the stove and, he suspected, from the strength of her emotion. He'd always loved Kate's warmth, the strength of her heart. It galled him to have to admit to himself that what she said held some truth. The thought flashed across his mind that the overwhelmed Bieler family had abandoned both Kate and Sarah.

Her hand resting on the table, she said in a tight voice, "When I married Jakob, I took Sarah as my own. I thought you were doing the same when you married me. But you've not tried to get to know her, at all. You've been standoffish and cold. It's no wonder she's nervous around you."

Silently staring at her, he knew she was right. Her apron was dusted with flour and a strand of her dark hair had escaped her bun to wisp from under her *kapp* to lie along her creamy neck.

Maybe it was foolish, but he...he loved Kate, even with all her untidy questioning. Even though she might not yet love him with all her heart.

In that moment, it was as if God spoke into his mind—any revenge he sought wasn't from the child. Kate was the one who'd rejected him—left him gasping in a fury and pain he'd never known. Maybe he had been less than welcoming to Sarah as an extension of that hurt.

Enoch cleared his throat before saying, "I have no Boppli. They are a mystery to me. I don't know how to get to know Sarah. I don't want to be her friend. Fathers aren't friends."

"No, and I don't wish you to try to be her friend. Just her father." Kate looked down at the table on which she'd rested her finger tips. "I think you could be a good father, Enoch. I think you will be a good father. You are a good man. I wouldn't have married you if I didn't believe that."

She probably wouldn't stay here with him, despite their marriage—or think that of him—if she read the letter from her uncle.

The brick in his stomach not easing, Enoch lowered his gaze. "Perhaps there is a little something in what you say. I'll—I'll try to get to know Sarah."

He looked up as he forced the words out, catching a glimmer of a relieved smile in Kate's eyes.

She dusted her hands on her skirt, her smile widening and she walked around the table, reaching her arms up to circle his neck as she leaned close. "Thank you, Enoch. I'm sure if you will let yourself, you will be a fine man."

Enoch sat on the porch in the dark of the evening after night had fallen. He was very aware that he and Kate hadn't resolved the issue of Sarah reading that book, but he had bigger battles to resolve. Somehow he had to become a father to Jakob Bieler's child…and be a good, Godly husband to Kate.

Around him the damp autumn wind whispered and sighed as he stared sightlessly toward his barn. In his haste to keep Kate from seeing her uncle's letter—at least until he'd thought about it more—he'd thrust the crackling piece of paper into a feed bin in the barn. Even though it was well hidden where Kate and little Sarah would never stumble on to it… and even with all the darkness around him now, he felt as if the letter glowed, like a green, evil thing. Signaling his deceit, tugging at him.

He wasn't one to gab a lot and he kept much to himself because it just made sense to do so, but Enoch liked plain-dealing. He was a straight ahead man…and yet the way here wasn't clear. All day since finding that letter in the mail, he'd struggled with what to do.

He didn't like secrecy. It tasted bitter in his mouth.

The evening chill sank in through his shirt, but he didn't move. Behind him the windows of his house glowed gently from the lamps and candles that Kate and Sarah used to light their clean up after supper.

Just the murmur of their voices—Kate's warm presence at his table. It made his house seem better, happier.

He'd lived alone in this house too long. Bitter with anger that the one woman he'd taken into his heart had left him—first for her *rumspringa* and then for Jakob—he'd lived here gladly by himself. Although he'd gone on, working the fields and sharing with family and neighbors, he'd never since been interested in any other woman. Other smiles had been sent his way; other girls in their community had grown into woman. But Enoch knew what fierce, soul-wrenching loss felt like. He hadn't been tempted once. Until now.

What did he do with that letter?

His head was muddled. All he knew was that he couldn't lose Kate now. He'd lost her once before, but he couldn't now.

Glancing again at the barn as if he could see through the timbers into the deep feed bin, Enoch wrestled with himself, guilt rolling in his stomach.

Straightening suddenly from his seat on the porch bench, he went to the front door and pulled it open. "Kate, I'm going to see my father. I'll be back later."

If anyone knew about loss, it was his widower father.

Tying his buggy horse up to the fence post near his dad's barn half an hour later, Enoch trod the path to the house through the cool night air. Having grown up here, his feet knew the way well. He reached the porch just as Isaac, his younger brother let the door shut behind him with a bang.

"Enoch! Are you visiting?" He looked around Enoch's shoulders. "Are Kate and Sarah with you?"

"No. I came alone." He climbed the steps to stand next to Isaac. "Are you going somewhere?"

His brother grinned a boyish smile. "Yep. Finished up that chair for *Daed*. Going to see my girl, now. I'd volunteer to stay and visit…but you know how it is."

Reaching to ruffle Isaac's head with a casual humor he didn't feel, Enoch said, "Go on, you *youngie*."

"Thank you. I will." His brother galloped down the steps and disappeared toward the barn.

Going into the house where the scent of wood smoke and familiarity greeted him, Enoch found his dad, sitting in a chair by the crackling warmth of the fire. Even after all these years since her death, his mind still envisioned his mother sitting across the fireplace from Samuel.

"Welcome, boy." Peering around him like Isaac had, his dad said, "You don't bring Kate with you?"

Enoch sank heavily into his mother's old rocker. "No. I didn't bring Kate, Father. I want to talk to you alone."

His father looked at him steadily, the fire in the fireplace hissing and crackling. "Go on, my son. You know you can always talk with me."

Suddenly feeling protective of Kate, Enoch didn't want to tell even Samuel about her having looked for asylum outside their world. It would have been considered a sadness, a shameful thing, by most in their world

His hands resting on his knees, he swallowed. "I—I sometimes have had vengeful thoughts toward Kate. Because she left me…and then married Jakob when she returned."

It was truth, although not all the truth.

In the warm shadowed light, his dad said gently. "Do you love Kate still?"

Sighing angrily, Enoch leaned back in his chair. He felt filled with rage and sorrow—all mixed together—but he couldn't have imagined not agreeing to Kate's proposal. If only the guilt sitting now in his stomach would ease. "It's not so simple, *Daed*. I love her, but…"

His father's smile was gentle, the fire behind him homey and familiar. "Son, marriage is complicated. This is why God counsels us to consider carefully before we take a mate."

"I know." Enoch flexed his hands against the chair's smooth armrests. "I prayed. A lot."

"*Acht!* Prayer is good. It is our request for God's guidance."

"*Daed*…" he wrestled with how to form the question, "…is it wrong to do something bad for a good reason?"

His father didn't respond immediately. "Enoch, I cannot know—and I do not ask—what bad thing you are referring to, but you know what God says is sin. He would want you to love your wife."

"I know, but forgiveness is not…easily given."

"You married her, Enoch." His *Daed's* voice was still gentle. "Is Kate not your wife now? No matter what happened in the past, you must forgive her even as our God forgives us."

"Yes…but, *Daed*, I am not nearly as wise and loving as He." Enoch had married Kate, offering both her and Sarah protection. But could he be sure he'd done it for a Godly reason?

Samuel chuckled. "No. And He doesn't ask us to be as wise and loving as He or expect that of us. You and Kate only married recently. Are there troubles already?"

"No." Enoch brushed a hand across his bare cheek and down over the husbandly beard that sprouted on his chin. "No. I—I like being married to Kate. She's a wonderful mother to Sarah…and a…good woman to me. A good wife."

I'm sure if you will let yourself, you will be a fine man. It was as if he heard her warm, loving words again.

His hand clenching against the rough texture of his every day pants, he drew in a deep breath, letting it out slowly to say again. "She's a good wife."

"Then, my son," his father's eyes, crinkled from hours in the sun, looked at him serenely, "you must remember that in the times when you think resentfully of the past. You love her and she is now your wife."

"Yes. She is." Enoch gazed across at his aging father, resolution settling in his chest. "Thank you, Dad."

He later drove his buggy through the night, reaching into his shirt to pull out the crumpled letter from Kate's uncle. She never needed to see it.

Stopping the buggy in a hollow down by a trickling brook, Enoch knelt at the water's edge and took out the worn tin that held his matches. She never need know.

Sitting on the wooden chair next to Enoch several weeks later, Kate glanced up at her husband, hiding a smile at the scraggly ruff of his marital beard. Enoch had been...warmer somehow, kinder since their argument over Sarah. A husband to Kate. He'd even spoken awkwardly to her daughter several times. Since the gruff, angry note was gone from his voice now, even Sarah seemed to have grown more comfortable around him.

Bishop Yoder sat at the front of the gathering, nodding occasionally when the preacher made a point.

After the service was over, Kate hurried to the kitchen to see if she was needed.

Handing out dishes and yeasty warm rolls later, she eventually found herself at the table where Enoch sat, his place down several from that of Aaron Yoder, the younger son of Bishop Yoder. As she used tongs to place a roll on the edge of each plate, she moved along behind the chairs, the men's conversation rising up.

She placed a roll on her brother-in-law Isaac's plate and moved around behind Enoch to reach over with her bread-laden tongs.

"...Yah, Brother Gunderson..." Aaron Yoder paused to swallow. "What you say about the Bible and women's roles is true. I think many women are uppity, particularly when it comes to what their jobs are in the family. I don't see they have anything to add to church doings."

Kate said nothing, stiffening as she paused ever so briefly in reaching past Enoch's broad shoulders. The blue jacket he wore was new. She'd just made it for him the week before and had been proud her mom had taught her how to make jackets to accommodate larger shoulders. With effort, she resisted the urge to run her hand along Enoch's shoulder. In her mind, she felt the power of him, though, the bunch of his muscles under the jacket she'd made for him.

She'd made her choice to stay in this life. Even though she had conflicts with the Aaron Yoders of the church.

"Women must learn," Aaron said with a shade of defiance, "that they're place is in the home, caring for the kinder and supporting what their husbands do."

Although her head was rigidly down—determined not to react to Aaron's ridiculous little-boy words-she was aware that Enoch's head had turned as he glanced up at her. Continuing to put the roll on his place, she grew conscious that her husband had reached over to tug on her skirt.

She met his warm brown gaze and saw understanding there. Tears of gratitude threatened and she glanced down again at the bread basket in her hand. Enoch's steady gaze brought warmth to her chest. He'd clearly heard the Yoder boy's words. She felt his gaze on her still as Enoch said, raising his voice just enough to be heard by those around him, "Aaron! Tell me if your mother helps your father. Has made his clothes and supports him in all he does as Bishop?"

Kate felt a smile curl the corner of her mouth as she went about her task, saying nothing. Her husband. He almost sounded as if he accepted her opinion. That he respected her opinion.

"Well...," Aaron stuttered into speech. "Yes, of course she makes our clothes."

"And helps around the farm, too?" Enoch's words were deep and unhurried. "Seems women have an important place."

She almost felt as if she would burst, having him so quickly stand up for—for women. And for her.

"Yes, but my mom doesn't tell my father how to be Bishop." Aaron's tone was a shade defensive, but he was clearly determined to make his point.

Kate moved on to place a roll on the plate of John Hochstetler who sat next to her husband. For once, John held his peace, looking back and forth between the Yoder boy and Enoch.

"Your mom also has a cheese business, doesn't she? And it makes money that goes into the family pot?" Enoch made his point so effortlessly, so without unpleasant confrontation. "And women vote for the church bishops. They help determine who will lead us."

She hoped, suddenly and fiercely, biting her tongue to keep from speaking—that he would somehow know how much his words meant to her.

"Of course, the money she makes goes into the family money."

Although Kate kept her head down, she could see from the corner of her vision that Aaron was now flushed and the tips of his ears pink. She'd been so right not to marry him.

So right to have humbled herself before Enoch as God had directed.

"And I believe she led the singing last church meeting, didn't she?"

Placing a roll on Aaron's plate, she stepped to the side, knowing Enoch could fight her battles.

"You know she did." Aaron spoke around the mouthful he'd shoveled in.

"Sounds to me," Enoch paused before going on, "that she's your dad's partner. Full partner. I don't know what we men would do without our helpmates…. Oh, that's right. You're not married yet. And your mom and dad are still helping you farm your new place."

Reaching now to put a roll on the plate of the man opposite Aaron Yoder, Kate glanced over. No matter how badly she'd felt about it when married to Jakob Bieler, she'd never stopped loving Enoch.

CHAPTER SIX

"Take Sarah with you." A week later, Kate stood next to the buggy, looking up at him as Enoch sat on the buggy seat.

"What?" he frowned down at her, shifting his hat back on his head, his simple trip to the village store for fall seed suddenly clouded. "I'm sure she'd rather stay here."

Around them, the air was crisp, leaving shadowed spots chilly and he was glad of his coat. Enoch held the worn leather reins in his hand, the brown gelding standing sedately in front of the buggy. The pale autumn morning light fell softly over the curve of his wife's face as she waited expectantly.

He looked over to where the child worked in the garden plot. "You have her pulling weeds. It's an important job. You need to get the vegetables planted."

"Enoch." It was said in a warning tone, as if he should know better than to push her.

Glancing back at Kate's beautiful face, set now with determination, he shifted the reins in his hands.

She lowered her voice. "We talked about this over a week ago. You said you'd be more of a father to her...and yet things between you two are pretty much the same. Take Sarah to the store with you."

"I am being more of a father to her. Have I said one more thing about that book she's reading?"

"No." His wife looked exasperated. "You haven't and you haven't said much to her, either. You need to step forward and act like her father. It is a God-given duty—to be a parent. You know

73

you are to love and be kind to her...since you've committed to be Sarah's parent. She still shies away whenever you're around."

"Kate," he spoke in lowered tones, as well, not wanting the child to hear them disagree. "Is that what a father must do? Take his daughter to the feed store? I don't think that's set out clearly in the Ordnung."

In truth be told he hadn't paid a lot of attention to what his own father had done with his sisters. Everyone did everything, including working the farm and sitting by the fire at night reading aloud as their mother sewed with neat stitches.

Of course, his mom had taught the girls to cut out and stitch clothes and to cook as Kate taught Sarah. Enoch didn't see where there was anything for him to teach her.

He had nephews and nieces and he loved messing around with them, but he somehow couldn't see himself wrestling with Sarah or carrying her on his shoulders. She was such a quiet child. It just seemed...not right.

"Fathers do lots of things with their daughters," the woman next to the buggy reminded him. "Why at service the other day, I saw you tickling your sister Lizzie's little girl."

"She's just a babe is Grace. Hardly four and I've known her all her life. You can't expect me to be the same way with Sarah all of the sudden. She doesn't even know me yet. I can't tickle her!"

"This is how Sarah needs to get to know you." Kate's jaw was set. "By doing things with you. Like going into town to buy fall seed."

"Kate, don't be silly."

"Take her with you." With the fire in her blue eyes, he knew Kate wasn't backing off.

"Fine." He gave in, frustrated and having no idea what he'd say to the girl. Enoch raised his voice. "Sarah. Sarah! Get your jacket. You're coming into town with me."

The girl in the new garden enclosure raised her head to stare at him, apparently as startled by the thought as was he.

"There," he told Kate. "Is that what you want?"

"Yes." She smiled up at him, a hint of complacency in the expression. "That's just what I want. You to find out you have the makings of a fine father."

Calling out to the girl still standing by the garden farrow, the surprised look still on her thin face, Kate said in a kind voice, "Go on, honey. Get your lighter coat. Enoch will wait."

"You don't expect her to call me father?" Enoch knew his lowered tone was sarcastic.

"Not yet," Kate shot back, "but I'd expect that eventually will be comfortable for you both."

Perversely, he had the urge to climb down from the buggy and kiss her senseless. He wouldn't, of course, because that sort of thing belonged in the bedroom and because he still wasn't sure of...anything about his feelings for Kate. Except that she was his wife now, in all definitions of the word. And he wanted to keep her that way.

Maybe he'd forgiven her and maybe he hadn't. But he still struggled...to completely let go of her rejection.

"Go back in the house, wife," he growled, feeling all mushy inside and resisting the reality. "I'm doing what you want."

The look she gave him as she turned back to the steps was saucy. "Thank you...husband."

The *clip clop* of the horse's hooves made the only sound as silence stretched out between Enoch and the blonde girl beside him in the buggy. The horse trotted in front of them—hitched just in front of the windshield—as he wrestled to find something to say. He knew more what to say to the horse, Old Bessie, than to Sarah.

She sat primly in her silence, the strings of her white prayer *kapp* fluttering in the fall breeze, plain sturdy shoes on narrow feet crossed at the ankle. For the life of him, Enoch could think of no way to converse with her. He wracked his brain.

Enoch shifted the reins in his hand as the buggy moved past rolling, fall meadows of wintering fields. Every now and then the autumn breezes kicked up the scent of the fields—dirt and freshly mown hay mixing with the lingering scent of rain.

"So, you and your mam have made a lot of progress in the vegetable garden."

The girl glanced at him, saying briefly, "Yes, sir."

"Kate said you're planting potatoes and beets and lettuces."

"Yes, we are." Even her voice sounded constricted. As if she thought he might bite her.

"Those will make for some good eating this winter," he said heartily. He had no idea if Sarah had known about Kate making him awful food in her pretense of not knowing how to cook, but he didn't see how that should be discussed. "I've always liked a good potato."

"Yes." Sarah just kept looking at the back of the horse through the buggy windshield.

Enoch let out a breath. He had no idea how to engage this child. He wasn't a big reader and she had to have overheard some of his conflict with Kate about her choice of reading material. It looked like this would be a long afternoon.

"So," he started again, lifting his voice some over the sound of the horse's hooves, "how is school going? Do you have lots of friends?"

Sarah glanced up quickly, before shifting her gaze again to Bessie's back. "I...guess. I mean, school and all of my classmates are fine."

He plowed ahead. "Do you have a favorite subject? I always liked arithmetic best."

Huddling her light jacket more tightly around her small frame in the fall coolness, Sarah said, "Oh, yes. Arithmetic is good."

"Your teacher is Miss Lapp?" He pushed forward, mentioning the older spinster who'd moved to the area several years back.

"Yes." The strings on Sarah's *kapp* bounced gently as she nodded.

Sending up a request to God to help him know how to engage with Kate's child, Enoch asked, "Do you like her? Is she fair?"

"Yes, she is." The small girl next to him said, "Miss Lapp lets me help her pass out books and sweep the schoolroom, sometimes."

As conversation went, this wasn't much, but he felt heartened a little by her volunteering anything. They were still a block or so from the feed store and he knew that as he'd given this some effort, he could now allow their talk to lapse. Grown-ups didn't have to interact with children, but he knew Kate loved Sarah and wanted him to make her welcome in their new home. Kate would want him to keep trying.

"So—I know you like to read," Enoch glanced over at the girl. "What do you like to read about mostly? When I was a boy, I liked looking at books that had pictures of animals."

Sarah looked up at him again. "I like reading about animals. And I like mysteries sometimes. Kate has given me the books she read as a girl, some were even passed down to her by her *Mamm*."

"Like the one you were reading last week." He could have ignored that subject completely, but he'd never been one to tippy-toe around things.

"Yes." The girl beside him kept her gaze on Bessie's broad brown back. "That was one of them."

"You and Kate lived with the Lehmans after your dad died. That book was once Elizabeth Lehman's, wasn't it?"

"Yes." The child gave a sudden, small sniffle." I miss Grandma and Grandpa Lehman. They were nice. I liked living with them."

The last part was said with a shade of defiance, as if Sarah thought he wouldn't like it. The corner of Enoch's mouth twitched. For some reason, he liked the *youngie* better for standing up to him a little.

"I liked them, too. I used to work with James—Grandpa Lehman—when he needed help on the farm."

She turned to look at him, as if this were news to her. "You did? I never saw you there."

"Yes. You must have been in school or inside the house helping your mother and Grandma Lehman when I was there.

Grandpa Lehman was my good friend." Enoch looked over at Sarah, his mouth turning down for a moment. "I miss James."

Turning to look back at the horse, Sarah said, "Me, too."

They continued on in silence a little ways and he realized the quietness between them had warmed a little. They had that in common anyway—their love of the Lehmans.

"Here we are," he said as they turned off the street into the feed store parking lot. Although there were *Englisch* customers' cars parked there at the feed store, Enoch also recognized the buggies of several of his neighbors.

He looped the carriage reins, leaving it parked over to the side out of the sun. Bessie deserved the best treatment and he didn't want her in full sun, even though the temps had dropped. Throwing a light cover across the horse's back to keep off the chill, Enoch told Sarah, "Come on in while I get the seed for next spring. Mrs. Yoder sometimes has cookies on a plate for customers."

"She does?" Sarah's face brightened as she hopped down from the buggy.

"*Ya*, and they're good cookies, too." He smiled at the girl, putting his hand on her thin shoulder to encourage her to go ahead of him.

Inside, Enoch quickly transacted his business, noting with amusement that Sarah had found both the plate of cookies for customers and Mrs. Yoder. The mother of a good size family and grandmother already to several others, he knew Mrs. Yoder loved *kinder*. While he finished up getting his seed from one of the Yoder's older sons, Enoch watched Sarah chatting shyly to Mrs. Yoder, even complimenting the woman on her oatmeal raisin cookie.

Enoch wasn't a fan of oatmeal raisin cookies, but it seemed Sarah was.

"Come on, *youngie*," he said, a big bag of seed balanced on his shoulder. "We don't want to keep Mrs. Yoder away from her other jobs."

"*Ya, ya*," the motherly woman smiled at them. "Come anytime."

"Thank you again." The girl gave her a big smile, "Particularly for the second cookie."

"You're so welcome. Come in with your *Daed*, anytime, sweetie." Mrs. Yoder beamed at her.

He shifted the bag higher on his shoulder, telling Sarah. "You should mention Mrs. Yoder in your prayers tonight, Sarah."

"Oh, I will." The little blonde carefully cradled her second cookie in a napkin as they moved toward the door.

They walked out and down the steps to the parking lot, heading over to where old Bessie was tied. The afternoon had grown a little chillier and as Enoch boosted Sarah onto the hard buggy seat, he paused.

"Here's a buggy robe for your lap. It's colder now."

The girl hesitated. "I'm okay."

"You won't be for long." He stuffed the buggy robe around her. "Here. Put this one behind you. That jacket isn't very heavy."

"Thank you." Sarah still held the cookie carefully.

Patting Old Bessie's nose as he went around to his side of the buggy, Enoch climbed onto the seat next to the girl.

They trotted out of the parking lot, starting down the street toward their farm and he glanced over. "Aren't you going to eat that cookie? Mrs. Yoder seemed to be happy you wanted it."

"She makes really good cookies," Sarah said with a reverence he found amusing. "I'm saving this for after supper."

"I'm sure that's just what your *Mamm* would prefer." Enoch glanced up at the lowering clouds. His buggy had a windshield, but he didn't want to drive back in either rain or sleet. "You can sit in the back, if you're cold."

"I'm fine. You wrapped me up warm." Sarah looked up at him, holding up the napkin-wrapped cookie. "Are you sure you don't want the cookie? It's really good."

His heart warmed by the child's gesture, he chuckled. "No, *youngie*. Save it for after supper. What did you think of the feed store?"

"I liked the way it smelled." Her nose wrinkled in her small face. "Like a mix of lots of things."

"Yes. Green things and fertilizer. I'm glad Mrs. Yoder keeps her cookies off to the back."

The horse trotted along a quieter side street after Enoch turned the buggy. The day had definitely grown chillier. He glanced over at Sarah, wondering how to keep her from being too cold on their ride back.

"There is smoke coming out of the Miller's chimney," Sarah said. "A lot of it."

He looked over at a big house on the hill to their left. "Yes. Green wood, probably."

As they moved along down the road toward their farm, he reflected that it was kind of nice not to make the trip on his own. Since he'd left his father's home and moved into his own place, he'd gotten accustomed to spending most of his days working by himself, except for the times he helped out with community raisings or he and James worked together on the older man's farm.

"Bessie is a nice horse, isn't she? I'll bet she never bites you." Sarah seemed reflective.

"No, not once," Enoch said with a tremor of laughter. "She's too smart as I'd have to school her, if she did."

"We had a farm horse at my dad's house—it was sold to support my Beiler grandparents—I think *Mamm* said they owned it. Anyway that horse was mean."

Smiling down at Sarah, he said, "Bessie is definitely not mean. She's gentle as can be. I don't really even have to tie her up. If I dropped the reins, she'd just stand there."

"Nice horsey," the girl ventured to say to the horse. Old Bessie's ears pricked back as if she knew Sarah were talking to her.

"Here." Enoch held out the reins to her. "You drive for a while."

She looked shocked and dismayed. "Me? I don't know how to drive a horse! I'm just a *scholar*."

"Old enough to drive Bessie. Come on," he said, gently taking her hand in his. "I'll hold your cookie. See? She's not even pulling at it. There. Just hold the reins in your hands. I'm right here if you need me, but Bessie is very well-behaved."

Sarah gulped, the leather reins now in her small hands. "I-I don't think I should."

"You're fine," he assured her, laughter again in his voice. "I wouldn't have you do it, if Bessie was likely to bolt. That would terrify us all."

"It's not…really all that hard, after all." Sarah still clung nervously to the leather reins he'd handed her.

"No." Sitting beside the girl, Enoch felt right. It was as if God had directed him to let her drive. "Would you like to learn to care for her? Bessie, I mean?"

He glanced over at the eight year-old girl, feeling as if something in him had shifted. This was something he would have taught any *Boppli* of his own. "I could teach you how."

Still holding the reins, Sarah turned a radiant face to him. "Really? You'd let me learn how to take care of her?"

It was as if the child knew absolutely how important this particular piece of livestock was to the farm. As if she got what a great trust caring for the horse meant.

"Sure. Of course, it means feeding her and learning how to buckle her harness and everything." Enoch glanced over with a small smile. "Even cleaning out her stall."

"I can do that."

The only time he'd ever seen that mulish determination on Sarah's face before was when she'd disliked him. Only this time, it wasn't dislike.

"I'll teach you then. Bessie will be yours and mine to take care of." He liked it, the connection between them.

"Good." The blonde child looked at him happily. "Oh, thank you."

Carefully ladling out the dinner stew later that afternoon, as the shadows gathered, Kate looked up when the door burst open and Sarah ran in with Enoch trailing behind.

"Oh, *Mamm*, oh, *Mamm*. I get to learn how to take care of Bessie. All by myself. Enoch's going to teach me." The child glanced back, "Aren't you, Enoch?"

"Yes, I am." Enoch smiled at Sarah, putting a hand briefly on her white-*kapped* head.

Warmth blossomed inside Kate like the flowers of summer, just seeing them like that. The wintery sound that had always been in his voice when he talked to her daughter before was gone now. Feeling the rush of moisture prickling behind her eyes, Kate smiled widely at them both. It was going to be alright. Everything was going to be alright.

Kate handed the wet dinner plate to Sarah later that night, perched on a chair next to the sink as the two of them cleaned up after dinner while Enoch took care of the evening chores in the barn.

"…he even let me drive Bessie," chattered the child as she dried the dishes before putting them in the cabinet. "And I let you taste the cookie from Mrs. Yoder. She said they're Mr. Yoder's favorites. I think we should ask for her recipe. I mean, your cookies are wonderful, but it never hurts to try new ones."

"No, we can never have too many cookie recipes," Kate teased.

Behind them, the front door opened and closed as Enoch came in. Feeling flushed as she glanced over her shoulder at him, Kate realized he carried something in his hands. Watching him come forward to lay a stack of books on the table, she met his eyes and noted a slightly sheepish expression there before his gaze skittered away.

"Sarah." He cleared his throat.

Having leaned forward to place the final washed dinner plate inside the cabinet, the girl then glanced back at him.

"I got these for you. From my *Da*." The tall, broad-shouldered man Kate had fallen for when they were teens seemed to feel a little awkward. "These were my *Mamm's* books."

Scrambling down from the chair, Sarah went to the table—and after carefully drying her hands again on her apron—opened the book on the top of the pile. "Your *Mamm*?"

"Yes." He came around the table, pulling another book from the pile. "You know she died a while back. You were just a babe then. You wouldn't remember her. But she was a reader—like your Grandma Elizabeth. She loved these. They're all about flowers and butterflies and animals—lots of pictures, too. I thought you'd like them."

"Oh…" Sarah's voice was reverent. "These are for me?"

Standing by the still undrained sink, Kate felt the beauty of the moment well up in her chest, thickening her throat and nose until tears started rolling quietly down her cheeks as she watched the two of them beside the table, Sarah turning the book pages with careful fingers.

It was as if the winter-chilled room had suddenly filled with God's love, flooding with a brightness and warmth Kate felt into her bones. Watching them, she sent up a prayer of thanks. This had to be His light, shining down into their souls.

Enoch was suddenly the father she'd always known he could be, treating her child—Jakob's child—with all the love she knew was in her husband. In that moment, she knew why she'd never stopped loving Enoch. Even through all the rough patches—times she'd never expected to be his wife—she'd known he was a good man.

The thunder rolled and crashed overhead later that evening as Enoch battled through the winds as he raced the short distance between the house and barn, rain slashing against his face and beat against the slicker covering his chest. The bad weather had rolled in fast while Sarah looked at his *Mamm's* books. He'd smelled the imminent rain earlier as he'd come back in the dusk from his father's house.

Automatically going out to check to make sure all in the barn was secure, he'd left Kate and Sarah inside. He needed to make sure everything was shut tight against the storm and that the animals were safe. Slamming the barn door shut against the wailing wind, he lit a lantern, making his way through the central area as he looked in on Bessie and the sturdy field horses in their stalls.

Bessie lifted her head from the hay he'd earlier put in her feedbox, her brown eyes wide with fear of the storm raging around them.

"You're alright, Old Bessie." The rain drumming on the barn roof, he reached over to pat the horse's warm flank, feeling that she was trembling a little. "You've been through storms before, girl. It's just rain."

As the words left his mouth, thunder crashed overhead and a bright sheet of lightening flashed through the crack around the stall's closed wood window. He patted Bessie's warmth again as he moved on to the work horses in the next stalls.

All while Enoch checked the other livestock, the noise of the storm raged and crackled around the barn. He took his time. If it was God's will that the barn blew away in the storm, he and his neighbors would rebuild and go about the business of this world. As he moved around in the building, checking that the pigs were safe under shelter and that the outside door to the attached chicken coop was secured, Enoch became aware of the sound of dripping water. It grew louder as he moved toward the back of the barn.

As he reached the last stall—empty at this time—he saw where the noise had been coming from, smelling the damp as he looked at the boggy mess there.

The blowing noise was louder here. Rain was dripping in and running down the wall in a glistening stream where roofing had blown off the corner of the barn. In the corner, where most of the leaking water had landed, the dirt floor around the cement corner pier had turned into a muddy quagmire.

Enoch placed the lantern on a nearby barrel, moving over to examine the damaged part of the roof.

Behind him just then, he heard the barn door blow open and looked back to see Kate inside the structure, wrestling to pull the door shut behind her.

"What are you doing out here? I thought you were staying inside with Sarah?" His words came out more sharply than he intended. Kate didn't need to be out in this. The wind wailed and he heard the rain drumming on the roof.

His lovely wife looked like a drowned rat, her prayer *kapp* drenched and a strand of her dark hair escaped from its bun to plaster against her cheek.

Coming over to the stall in the corner, she responded to his question almost absently. "You were out here so long. Sarah's fine. She's reading the books you gave her. What's going on? Do we have a leak?"

He stared at her a moment, wavering between the urge to send her back to the safety of the house and the knowledge that doing so would seem like a rejection. Besides…he found his mood lightening with her presence.

"The corner of the barn roof blew off and it's raining in on that part. It's weakening the corner foundation post."

"Gosh!" She stepped around him, picking up the lantern to shine it on the exposed roof boards where the rain still blew in. "What do we do?"

Enoch's chest rose, warmth from her inclusion seeping through him. "I have to go out and put oilcloth on it, I guess. There has to be some protection against the rain getting in and messing more with the corner footing."

She shifted the lantern, looking at the wet boggy floor at the corner. "Yes, but how do we get the corner covered? Even if we put it up on the inside at the roof-level, the rain will still come in. Do we just get buckets and wait till morning to fix the roof? Wait. Did you say you plan to go out and fix it now?"

"Yes. And no, we can't patch it from the inside." Enoch left the stall, going to the other side of the barn where he found a bucket in which to place some of the nails. They clanged as he placed them inside.

Still holding the lantern, Kate followed him. "What are you doing?"

"Fixing the roof."

"You're going out now? In this storm?" Concern sharpened her words and she followed as he went to where the ladder hung sideways on the barn wall.

"Kate, you know I can't wait."

"It's thundering and lightning." She put a slender hand out to clutch at his bicep. "Let the repair wait!"

He sighed with exasperation. "You know it can't wait."

"And if the lightning strikes you?" Her voice came more strident. "I won't be widowed Enoch. Not again...and not with you."

Lightning flashes played with the shadows on her tight features as the storm raged outside.

"I'll be okay." He unhooked the ladder from the wall, the last part of her remark making his insides squishy. "There's a sheet of oilcloth in that bin. Get it for me."

"What do you mean? You'll be okay." She went to drag out the yellow water repellant cloth, although clearly not on board with his intent. "You can't know you won't be struck by lightning, Enoch."

"Katie, the leak must be fixed. God will be with me." He leaned the ladder against a stall to shrug his slicker together.

She stood watching him, saying with sudden determination. "I'm going out to help you."

"What!" Enoch's head snapped up from his job. "No, you're not. Don't be silly."

She moved over to hoist the ladder over her shoulder, stepping forward with a mulish look on her pale face.

He looked at her, his mouth twitching with an urge to laugh, despite the situation. "Now, what are you going to do out there? Climb the ladder with me?"

"No." Her glare was withering. "I'm going to hold the bottom in place while you climb up there—fool that you are. The ground is muddy and slippery. That way if you slip on the ladder, I'll break your fall."

"Are you crazy? I'm not falling on you. And you aren't going out in this." He stood glaring back at her, feeling no urge to laugh now. "Tacking the oil cloth over the hole won't take me a minute. I promise I'll come right back inside."

Kate stepped closer, dragging the ladder with her. She met his gaze, saying in a deadly voice, "If you go out, I'm going out with you. I'm your wife and it's my barn, too."

"While we are standing here arguing," his frustration made him sound annoyed, he knew, "more and more rain is pouring in. Just stay here inside."

"If you go out," she repeated in that same flat, determined voice, "I go out."

He dropped the nail bucket to the straw-littered floor. "You must know I can't let you go out in the storm. I've promised to take care of you. What kind of a husband would that make me?"

Her blue gaze pierced him. "What kind of a wife would let you go out alone to do this? We're in this together. My barn, my husband."

Enoch held her gaze, registering that all his arguments weren't turning her. Trying one more time, he said, "You're not dressed for this."

"Then get me a slicker and let's get to it."

Reluctantly, he reached over and snagged another slicker from the nail where it hung. "You're sure? You're leaving Sarah inside alone."

"You said God will protect you. I'm sure He'll do the same for me and Sarah."

His brows lifting as Enoch reached over to pull a hammer from a peg, he knew he couldn't argue with that.

"Okay." He turned back to her, dropping the hammer into the bucket before reaching up to fling the slicker around Kate's slender form. "Tie all the fasteners. It'll be big, but that may help keep the wet out. There's a hood."

Not waiting for her to do as he'd said, Enoch began threading Kate's arms into the slicker, tying the garment around her clumsily, at her wrists and her neck with the hood cord secured under her chin. "You're skirt will get wet."

"Yes." She smiled at him as he worked to secure the slicker, her mouth seeming to tremble some.

He thrust his arms into his own slicker, yanking it together. "Come on, Katie girl, and you'd better pray I don't slip and land on you."

He grabbed the wooden ladder from Kate and headed toward the barn door, their slickers rustled noisily. Enoch wrenched open the door, wrestling to keep the wind from ripping it out of his hands. The scent of the storm enveloped them. Hitching the ladder more securely over his shoulder, he held the bucket in one hand, reaching his other hand out to take Kate's.

The cool wind and rain roared around them as they stepped into the night, the trees gyrating wildly in the storm. The sound of it was so loud, no words they'd spoken could have been heard. The ground under their feet was thick with drenched grass and he almost immediately felt the wet sink in through his work shoes and woolen socks. Leading Kate in a darkness only lit by flashes of lightening, he held close to the barn wall, sheltering as much as they could from the buffeting rain. The wind was so strong, Enoch reflected as they side-stepped along the wall, it was as likely to blow him off the ladder as the rain was to make his foot slip.

Getting to the end of the barn wall—right at the corner with the damaged roof, Enoch gestured to Kate for her to step over the river of mud that now streamed under the barn wall from the rain pouring inside. At least the crashing lightening allowed her to see him. They turned the corner to the barn's end wall and he then pressed Kate back against the barn, gesturing for her to stay there, sheltered a little under the overhang, while he set up the ladder, the uneven light making it harder. The wind howled more intensely from this direction.

Although the wind made moving the ladder into position even more of a challenge, he managed to get it into place. As he reached into the bucket for the oil cloth to nail over the damaged area, he realized Kate had stepped further out into the storm. He didn't think there was any need, but she clearly intended to brace the ladder he had to climb. As he stepped on the lower ladder rung, it sank into the softened muddy ground and it occurred to him that maybe having her hold the thing in place wasn't a bad idea.

With the rain blowing into his eyes, Enoch ducked his head. Since his hat would have blown off in the storm, he'd left it in the house earlier and the rain now plastered the slicker to his head. The oil cloth clamped under one arm, the bucket gripped tightly in his hand, his other hand braced against the wooden ladder as he climbed. The storm raged over head, the heavens crackling with flashes of lightening as thunder rumbled around them.

In short time, he was eye-level with the corner of the barn roof that had blown open. The wind was stronger here. Leaning forward carefully to maintain his balance in the gusting rain, Enoch braced the bucket between the tilted ladder and the side of the barn, fighting the wind to open the folded oil cloth.

"Are you okay up there?" Kate called out, her voice strained to reach above the noise blowing around them.

"I'm good." He focused on the job in front of him, urgent to get Kate in out of the storm.

The rain made the nails slippery in his hand as he stuffed the metal spikes between his teeth. Knee pressed against the bucket, Enoch managed to hold the flapping oil cloth against the barn roof with one elbow, while he secured it roughly over the sloping open frame timbers.

Shifting back a little, he stepped down the lower ladder rung to nail the oil cloth to the side of the barn.

With Enoch working up on the ladder, Kate pressed herself against the lower rungs in the darkness, hoping her body weight would keep the ladder in place. Her head lowered against the

89

raging storm, she prayed furiously, ignoring the cold sodden skirt whipping around her ankles.

God, please keep Enoch safe. Put Your hand over him and shelter him against this awful storm.

When Jakob had died, she'd felt stunned with sorrow at his life suddenly cut short...but she didn't think she'd be able to draw breath if something happened to Enoch.

She felt the ladder vibrate with his movements above her and knew the moisture on her face wasn't only the rain.

Long aching minutes past, the slicker flattened against her chilled body by the wind and rain, before she began feeling the rhythmic tremble of the ladder that signaled Enoch was descending. The sodden lower half of her dress hampering her movement, Kate slithered to the side, keeping her hands gripped to the wet ladder as he climbed down.

"Come on!" he yelled when he thrust the bucket at her, yanking the ladder forward to hoist it.

She followed him along the barn wall as he moved toward the door, the rain still slashing at them.

Enoch having stowed the ladder in the barn, he hustled Kate through the still-blowing storm into the house. Sarah looked up from her book in mild surprise as they stood in front of the closed door, him untying the slicker.

"Are the animals all right?" An oil lamp gleamed on the table next to her book. "Oh, you're all wet."

"Yes," Kate answered the girl, her teeth chattering a little.

"We had to cover a corner of the barn roof that had blown off," Enoch said, still working at untying the slicker that huddled around Kate. "You're *Mamm* insisted on holding the ladder while I fixed the roof temporarily."

"You c-could h-have slipped," she said, through lips that quivered. Even though the fireplace and wood stove kept the house toasty against the weather, her cold, wet dress still clung to her and chilly water trickled down her neck from the slicker hood, now thrown back.

"Can you get yourself ready for bed?" Enoch turned to look at the girl. "It's past your bedtime now, isn't it? Your *mamm* needs to get warm."

Closing her book over a sliver of bookmark, Sarah started getting up. "Of course. Do you need help, *Mamm*?"

Before she could answer, Enoch said, "That's alright, child. I'll tend to her. You just get yourself to bed."

Teeth now chattering in earnest, Kate said, "I can do it. I don't need tending."

"You are cold," he loosened the last knot on her slicker, "because you insisted on holding the ladder. You need to get into a warm bath."

As he pulled the dripping slicker from her shoulders, she protested, "I don't need a bath, Enoch. Just warm clothes. You know it's a mess."

His hands on her shoulders, he turned her. "You are the most difficult woman I know. I'm setting up a bath now with warm water. Go in the bedroom and take off your wet things."

"I just need to sit by the fire—I mean, yes. Take off the wet clothes, but after that I'll be fine."

"Will you listen to me just once, woman?" Enoch braced his broad hands on his hips, his lips curving into a smile she hadn't seen in years. "You held the ladder for me. The least I can do is make you a warm bath."

Kate saw Enoch turn off the hot water in the bath as she stepped into the bathroom. Her heart swelled within her as he reached over with a strong, tanned hand to froth the soapy water.

"There," he said, glancing over one broad shoulder as she came into the room, "I think it's warm enough. Test this."

Reaching down, she hugged her robe more tightly across her chest, dipping her fingers in the bath water. "Yes, it's just right."

The rain could be heard still pelting on the house's roof and she felt a deep sense of warmth and connection that together, she and her husband had secured their barn against the elements.

"Okay." He looked around the small room. "You have towels. We don't want you catching cold, getting out of the bath. Bad enough that you were out in that chilly rain."

"There are two towels on the shelf," she nodded toward them.

"Good." Enoch straightened, shaking his damp hand over the full tub as he smiled at her. "We don't want you sick. I mean, Sarah's used to your cooking and making do with mine would be a hardship on her."

Just like it always had, Enoch's smile sent a bolt straight through her. He hadn't smiled at her much through the years, not even a lot since their marriage. She felt warmed into her bones that he did now.

"Okay," he moved to the bath door. "Don't stay so long you get cold."

Kate's breath came more quickly. They'd been man and wife and slept in the same bed now for over a month, but there still had seemed a wall between them. Now that wall seemed to have crumbled some. She was so very glad.

Watching as he opened the door and started through it, Kate said in a low voice, "Enoch?"

He stopped, looking back at her, his brows raised in question.

"Stay." She felt her voice wobble a little. "Stay with me."

For a moment, he was frozen there, his gaze locked with hers. For long seconds, they looked at one another, Kate trying to communicate through her expression. She loved Enoch. She wanted him to know how much.

"Stay with me," she repeated.

CHAPTER SEVEN

Several weeks later, sitting at the back of several rows of chairs in the house in which her parents had raised her, Kate reached out a hand to her friend. Hannah sank into the chair next to her in the chairs set aside for the women, baby Lydia cooing and babbling in her arms. The meeting hadn't started yet and the neighbor women who sat around her chatted together amid the fragrance of the cooking lunch that would be served later.

"Hello, friend." Kate shifted to face her very pregnant friend, still holding Hannah's strong, warm hand. "How do you feel? You look as if you aren't sleeping well."

"*Ya*. Well, that's just natural at this point. I'm doing fine." She shifted Lydia. "It must be strange to be back in this house."

Kate glanced around, noting the serviceable furniture and plain rug that had been added. The Troyers had changed little things, but most everything was still the same. Plain houses never had much ornamentation as it would be both unnecessary and boastful. "It is strange to come back here."

The house even smelled the same—of her mother's cooking and her father's soap. "I keep expecting to see my mother stirring a pot of stew in the kitchen."

Hannah gave her a sympathetic glance, jiggling Lydia on her knee. "Yes, of course. That is the hardest. We know the loved ones who have passed on are in the hands of God and therefore fine, but we still miss them."

Kate felt herself tearing and blinked back the moisture as she looked down at her lap. It was the way of their life not to display emotion, a reality her mam had tried to instill in her all of Kate's life. She spoke in lowered tones. "That is the hardest. I miss them so much. This house brings it all back to me."

As Enoch, Kate and Sarah had ridden over in the buggy, he'd silently reached out to squeeze her hand when they'd turned into the drive. He must have known that coming back to this house would be hard for her. Thinking of him now—his rough, calloused hand gripping hers—brought a warm flush to her chest, remembering how close they'd become in the last little while. Ever since fixing the barn in the storm.

Kate flashed a glance across the room at him, sitting on benches with the other men.

"It is getting a little easier. Having a family of my own to look after helps."

"*Ya.* I understand that." Hannah shifted baby Lydia to her other knee.

"We haven't had a chance to talk since last meeting." She smiled at Hannah, reaching for the warm, wiggling baby.

"I know." Her friend responded with an engaging grin that made her seem too young to have a growing family. She handed chubby, cuddly Lydia to Kate. "Two weeks sometimes seems like forever. How have you been?"

Hannah lowered her voice and leaned closer. "Is everything going okay? I mean, with Enoch and all?"

A laugh stumbled out of Kate and she glanced around casually before leaning closer herself, using the baby's warm form as a privacy shield as she responded softly to Hannah. "Oh, so well. I've—we've—been doing very well."

Hannah's smile widened as her eyes opened in surprise. "Really? Tell me."

"It's like," Kate said, dropping her voice even lower, "before. Like when we were courting."

To have him back—the Enoch she'd first loved—made her almost giddy with relief.

"Oh, I know how much you've longed for that! Ah, I told you he loved you still," her friend exclaimed.

"*Shhhh!*" She tucked Lydia under her arm as she patted Hannah's hand, unable to keep her own smile from growing.

"So, Enoch has finally forgiven you for marrying Jakob?" the woman hissed, her frizzy, blonde curls peeping under her *kapp*.

Pretty much whispering now, Kate said, "I think so."

They were moving forward beyond the difficult times that had come between them too long. The memory still brought pain to her midsection. Kate shivered a little, suddenly aware of the winter winds howling around the house.

"This is good," Hannah whispered back.

Kate handed the baby a carved wooden rattle, reflecting that that the months surrounding her *rumspringa* had been a horrible time. She'd felt more for Enoch in the early months of their courtship than she'd ever known possible, even telling him of her doubts and questions about the lifestyle. While he'd not seem terribly disturbed by her frustration that women weren't allowed some roles in the church, he'd gotten angry when she decided several months later to go to her uncle in Baltimore.

Going anyway—despite his ridiculous edict—had seemed very necessary. Perhaps even more so than before Enoch laid down the law. How dare he act like he could boss her around! She'd fallen for him hard during their courtship and hadn't questioned that she wanted to marry him, but everything had changed when she started talking about going to Baltimore.

Several chairs down and a row or two in front of her, Lizzie, one of Enoch's sisters, sat with her toddler, Grace, beside her. When Lizzie caught sight of Kate behind her as she looked over her daughter's prayer-*kapped* head, she smiled and raised her hand in a silent wave.

Kate smiled back, nodding at her sister-in-law. From the first when they'd been youngies courting, Enoch's family had welcomed her warmly. This hadn't changed, even with her having married Jakob, about which she'd been a little startled and very relieved. Across the room, Kate saw his father, Samuel, sitting on the same bench beyond Isaac and Enoch. She liked the Miller family, feeling really sad when Ruth, Enoch's mother, had passed.

Looking across the room at Enoch now, all their courtship turmoil seemed like such a long time ago—but the feelings for him had never left her heart. Even when she'd been so angry at him, so hurt that he hadn't written.

Even after she'd married Jakob…to her shame.

The bishop had come to the front of the meeting then and the buzzing voices around them started quietening as the sermon began.

"Later," Kate murmured to her friend as Hannah's mouth opened to speak. Thoughts of that dark time with the man she'd loved so dearly—and thought she'd lost—only made this reconnection with Enoch more joyful.

The lengthy sermon continued most of the morning with Bishop Yoder surprising many by yielding the floor after his sermon to his youngest son, Aaron. The Bishop had spoken at length about congregants showing their love for God by their actions, their avoidance of pride and boasting—most of this the usual talk for sermons given to the plain folk.

During the sermon, she and Hannah had quietly taken turns tending baby Lydia.

Although Sarah had come inside the house at the beginning of the sermon to sit to the side, whispering quietly with several other young girls, Kate was startled to see her later seated next to Enoch.

She'd felt a smile automatically curve her mouth at the sight.

Kate had already started thinking of how she could help out with serving the lunch meal when Aaron Yoder stepped forward after his father's sermon.

"It is written," he said with a seriousness that almost seemed comical given his age and the fact that there were other elders present, "that men and women have different jobs in the family."

Kate felt herself stiffening as he glanced her way with some significance, a flush of anger starting in her chest.

"Men are to be the leaders in the family and the church. This is our way and God's way."

Hannah and John's older daughter, Rebecca, had woven her way through the chairs and now leaned against her mother. Kate absently put her arm around the girl.

"God has given us these roles and it is prideful for anyone to question the natural order of things…"

Prideful!

It was one of the worst things that could be said of anyone in their lifestyle. The slow burn in her chest notched up several degrees. This was the attitude that frustrated her most about the church.

As best she could, Kate blocked out the next hour of Aaron's talk. He sometimes shifted into prayer—as speakers often did—beseeching God to be with them and help His children to be faithful followers, which included staying in the established roles—men as the leaders, women bearing and raising the children, as well as, maintaining the home.

Seated across the room from Kate, Enoch sat through Aaron's prayers, concerned that his wife heard all the barbs sent her way and noted Aaron's pointed looks at her. It was clear that her rejection of Aaron—and her comments at the last worship meal—had started a vendetta on the side of Bishop Yoder's youngest son.

Watching Kate's face whiten and then flush during the last part of the sermon, he was startled as Sarah—who'd surprised him by coming to sit next to him—slipped her warm hand in his. She held her doll in the crook of her other arm, sitting quietly next to him.

Enoch's fingers curled around Sarah's smaller hand as he quickly swallowed the sudden lump in his throat. Jakob Beiler's child was becoming Kate's child to him. And more. Sarah seemed increasingly like herself. Like a child he could love as his own.

Across the room, he saw that Kate held the Hochstetler's baby while Hannah leaned forward to talk quietly to their older girl. Although she jiggled the infant comfortably, he could tell his wife wasn't happy with what the Yoder boy was saying. Kate had never been good at hiding her thoughts.

The last part of the morning preaching—Aaron's part—was finally over and Enoch could only be glad that Kate didn't have to listen to any more. As the members of the congregation rose and started moving around the bustle of chatter and scrape of chairs rising, Sarah sat next to him still, drawing on a scrap of paper against her knee—baby doll held in her crooked arm.

He saw Kate almost immediately moved to the kitchen of the home—the house she'd been raised in—to help with the meal as the men of the group moved benches and chairs to make room for the tables on which their meal would be served.

Never had Enoch been more conscious of the letter from Kate's Uncle Brandon. A sense of guilt gathered in his throat, even though he knew he had justification for what he'd done. He'd strangely grown to feel as if that letter existed still, although he knew he'd burned it by the brook that evening.

It didn't matter, he told himself. Even if her Uncle Brandon had finally responded, Kate was married—committed, promised—to him now. His wife.

The last part of the sermon this morning hadn't helped, though. This was what Kate hated about the lifestyle, this kind of talk that proclaimed such tight restrictions on what women of faith did. This was why she'd talked of leaving the Amish way of life.

He felt sick in his gut.

Murmuring now to Sarah to prod her to shift her activities outside the bustling area, Enoch ran a troubled hand through his hair. He had married Kate—pledged his life to be loyal to her, to live by her side and allow her slowly worm her way back into his cautious heart—but he knew she still harbored questions. The fact troubled him, just as the possibility that she'd somehow find out what he'd done with her letter.

Two days later Kate wiped her hands on the damp kitchen towel, surveying the stack of clean dishes on the shelf with approval.

Although the month of December had progressed, the day had dawned that morning with bright sunshine and a surprisingly mild temperature. The last warm days of the fall had come late. Although Sarah had helped clean off the table, she'd been whining for the last hour that she needed to go outside the house to do her other chores.

Kate had finally agreed, knowing her daughter would end up feeding apples and corn to the mare in the barn. She and Bessie were becoming close friends ever since that day when Enoch let the child drive the buggy.

Still startled by the warmish breeze that drifted through the windows, Kate turned to take a broom from a nearby corner, planning to sweep any stray crumbs from the floor.

Through the open window, she heard Sarah's childish treble as she called to the chickens to come get the feed she scattered. The bang of Enoch's hammer could be heard as he finished the last of his repairs to the barn roof.

Kate smiled to herself, the thought of her husband leaving a pleasurable flush of heat in her chest. She still felt guilty about being happy with him when she'd never truly felt that way with Jakob.

But she liked her life now—particularly the parts with Enoch and Sarah. With them and friends like Hanna and even Lizzie, she couldn't see wanting to be somewhere else. That had never really been her thought, even with her questions about some aspects of their assembly. *Rumspringa* was the Amish way to allow their children to clearly choose the *Englischer* world or this life of worship. Although she hadn't considered leaving the faith, she'd almost done worse in being frustrated with the Amish limitations on women. She wanted to change it. At least, many appeared to think this was worse. In her eyes, the Ordnung had evolved to preserve the best way to live the life of worshipping God. What had evolved could grow some more as long as the order of Godly life wasn't shaken.

She couldn't help thinking again about Aaron Yoder and those who thought like him, her mouth turning down. If only those afraid of change realized that their world wouldn't suffer if women were allowed to profess their love of God in more ways than having babies and raising small farm animals.

Sweeping up the wooden kitchen floor, she then got out the mop and bucket to scrub it all. When she was on her knees in the corner of the kitchen later, she thought she heard the jingle of a buggy bridle, but since she was in the middle of her work—and no one came to the door—she ignored the sound she thought she'd heard through the open window.

"Kate!"

She lifted her head when she heard Enoch's voice call her name.

"Kate! Come out here!"

Getting to her feet and drying her hands on the dish towel again, she grabbed a sweater and went to the door, stepping onto the porch. "What is that?"

Hatless and stocky in his shirtsleeves in the cool air, his suspenders over broad shoulders, Enoch stood on the buggy path in front of the house, a wheeled contraption propped in his hands. A bicycle. She knew what he held because she'd seen *Englischers* riding sleek, highly-modern versions.

"Come, woman!" He grinned at her. "I got you a bicycle."

Slowly crossing the porch to descend the steps, Kate said, "Enoch, are you crazy? Why do I need one of these? Besides I've never ridden one! I wouldn't know how."

He shifted as she came closer to the contraption, his big hands now gripping the handles. "You can learn. I got it from old John Lappe when I was at the feed store last time. He said he'd gotten it from a cousin over at Haddington Mills, thinking his wife could use it—and get moving some."

Circling him and the blue bicycle, Kate rested her hand on the chrome handles, looking it over. The bicycle frame dipped where her skirt would fall and seemed clean, even if it looked a little scary.

"But his wife totally refuses to use it! Hasn't even touched it in months. He just decided to get rid of the thing, since she won't ride it. I snapped it up for you."

"But why?" She eyed the contraption cautiously.

"You can learn to ride it. You don't have to harness the buggy for shorter trips. You don't have to wait if I need Bessie in the fields. Here, just step over it." He urged her to step over the frame.

"Enoch," Kate said in a scolding voice, "I'm not a *youngie*. I'm past learning how to handle this contraption. "John Lappe's wife was right."

"Don't be ridiculous. Miriam Lappe is fifty, if she's a day, and she carries significantly more weight than you. You're trim and lovely."

Although unsure that she could balance on the bicycle, Kate flushed with pleasure at his description of her. "But Enoch...I don't think I can ride it. There are only two wheels and I don't know how to balance it. I mean I've seen some others do it, but..."

"Not a problem." He braced the front wheel between his legs, both hands on either end of the handle bars. "Climb on while I hold it steady—just to get the feel. Then, we can go out to the road. I run next to you while you peddle and get your balance. I once saw an *Englischer* friend do that with his sister."

"Ooookay." Kate stepped astride the contraption, her long skirt brushing against the dip in the frame. "Are you sure?"

"Yes." Enoch's strong reply certainly sounded sure.

Kate positioned her rear end on the small seat, squealing when Enoch shifted his feet, the bicycle moving a little.

"I've got you. Are you on it securely?" His feet were braced wide apart as he held the frame, grinning at her.

"I-I think so, but I think I'll fall over if you aren't holding it." Kate felt tall, sitting on the bicycle. "You're enjoying this too much. I think you just want to see me go sprawling."

"Don't be silly. You won't fall if you're moving. Put your feet on the pedals there. Yes, that's right. Now, hop off and we'll go down to the road."

She walked next to him as he pushed the bicycle down their drive, the insects in the wintering fields silent now. "I don't see how this is going to work. It's alright. I use the buggy when I need to and I actually like walking."

"You can still walk sometimes, but this will give you a choice besides Bessie, who I sometimes use in the fields. See? It has a basket right here on the handle bars and you can carry small things in it, if you need to run errands."

The bike's rubber tires crunched against the ground as he rolled it and Kate felt herself growing excited.

Walking through the gate at the end of their drive, his feet scuffing through piles of leaves, Enoch positioned the bicycle in the road, motioning for her to get on. "Here. See? I'm holding it. That's right, climb up on the seat."

Kate nervously braced her hands on the handle bar grips and scooted up on the seat Enoch held for her. Looking down, she placed her sturdy shoes on the pedals and looked up at him. "You aren't going to let go until I'm ready?"

"Absolutely." He nodded his brown head in the direction the bike faced. "Just start off."

"What? Just move the pedals?"

"Yep, and I'll run next to you."

Shifting her feet on the pedals as he braced her on the bicycle, she swallowed and said, "Okay. I think I'm ready."

"Good. Start moving your feet around in circles on the pedals."

She found when she pushed on them, the bicycle started moving forward, Enoch beside her. "Oh, my!"

Carefully, moving her feet and the pedals more quickly with him trotting alongside, holding the back of the bicycle seat.

"Eeeeek!" Startled by the increasing rush of fall air past her cheeks and her rapid movement forward, without realizing what she was doing, Kate took her hands off the handle bars, grasping for the broad shoulder security that ran next to her.

"Kate! Kate! Put your hands back on the handle bars!"

Even as she heard him yell, she felt the bicycle begin to wobble under her. "Enoch! *Aaiieee!!!!*"

The wobble turned into a tilt from which they couldn't recover, the bicycle hurtling them into the culvert along the roadside. Kate screamed as the ground of the ditch came up to meet her out-stretched arm. Spilling over ungraciously—the bicycle tangling in her long skirt—she felt the damp wild grass under the hand she put out to catch herself. As she fell, she realized that rather than let go of the bicycle to save himself, Enoch had somehow stumbled forward with her, shoving the machine ahead a little of her and only managing to keep from landing on her with his full weight by putting out his own hand and rolling to the side.

The smell of crushed grass was sweet around them.

Still jumbled and dazed by the spill, she realized Enoch—his big body pressed to her side—was shaking with laughter. She looked over in astonishment. "Enoch! What are you laughing about? We just crashed this silly thing. This is terrible. I-I was just so surprised, I—"

"I'm sorry," he offered between chuckles that he was clearly trying to suppress, "are you okay?"

He straightened from her, scanning her body. "Did you sprain anything? Scrape anything?"

The fact that he was still grinning broadly—despite obviously trying not to—had Kate herself smiling in response. "How can you laugh at this?"

"Are you hurt?" He stood, pulling the bicycle upright to free her legs.

"I don't think so, not to be concerned about anyway."

He started chuckling again, "Oh, Kate. If you could only see yourself."

Making a face at him, she put up a hand to straighten her askew *kap*p. It was then that she noticed the trickle of blood on his wrist."

"Oh, my! You're hurt! Enoch, let me see!" She felt horrible, very aware that it was her own silliness in letting go of the steering bars—and needing to be taught how to ride in the first place—that had led to his injury.

Twisting his wrist casually, he looked at his scrape, wiping the blood away on his pants leg as he said, "Huh. It's alright. Here, let me help you up and let's try it again."

"Again!?" She was a strong woman, but she'd never been good at forgiving her own mistakes. "It's fine. I don't need to ride."

"Yes, you do." He stretched out his hand for hers. "You can do this. It was just a little tumble. Come on."

"That was a little tumble?" She got up, straightening her skirt.

"Nothing is broken. Let's do this."

"If you insist."

"I do." By this time, he'd lifted the bicycle—none the worse for the crash—out of the ditch and now held his hand out to hoist her up.

"Okay, but I could damage you even more, I'm such a klutz." She took hold of the strong hand he offered and scrambled forward.

"Don't be silly. You can do this." He again held the bicycle still while she clambered onto it, her feet on the pedals. "Now this time, hang onto the handle bars. Yes, grip them good, they will give you balance and you'll need to lean a little in the direction you want to turn, once you get your balance."

For the next half hour, Enoch ran up and down the road in front of the house, his hand holding the bicycle as she rode, eventually she began to feel the balance of riding it. She felt proud that they had only one more crash, not as bad this time and not because she took her hands off the handle bars.

Panting as he came to a stop beside her, Enoch said between breaths, "Okay. I think you're getting it. Ready for me to let you go? I almost did it that last run."

"You're letting go?" She hated feeling like such a baby.

"Well, I hadn't planned on always being there to run beside you," he said, still gasping in air.

"Fine. You can let go this time." She looked at him with beady eyes. "But not until I'm ready. You don't let go until I tell you."

"I won't," he said, "but I may die if it takes too long."

"Then you'll have a good reason to let go of me."

Enoch started laughing again. "You can be a hard woman, Kate Miller."

"Just remember that," she said to him as she slowly started pedaling with him walking faster beside her. By this time, they'd traveled down the road a ways from the house. She firmed her mouth with determination and directed him, "Let's go faster. I'm getting it this time."

As he ran beside her, she pedaled, feeling the balance as she leaned a little one way and the other. "Now! Let go now!"

In her exhilaration at shooting forward on the bicycle, she didn't realize for a moment that Enoch was no longer running beside her. She rode on further down the road, slowing to carefully negotiate a U-turn at a neighbor's gate, pedaling her way back to him.

He stood in the road, smiling at her as she rode up to him. "There you are. I said you could do it."

She was so thrilled with her accomplishment, she jumped down to walk the bicycle over to him, planting a kiss on his cheek. "Thank you, Enoch. Thank you for getting this for me and for helping me learn how to ride it."

"You're welcome." He turned to walk beside her as they headed back toward their land, the bicycle between them. "Now, I think we should buy one for Sarah."

Casting a glance up at him, Kate said with hesitation, "A bicycle? Do you think so? She's just getting comfortable driving the buggy behind Bessie when you're with her. Do you think she's old enough to learn how to ride a bicycle?"

"Yes, I do. I was younger. I haven't had one for a while, but learning now will be good for her," he pronounced, looking over at her.

Smiling and hugging close the happiness she felt with the parental note in his voice, she said, "Good, then. Whenever you can find a bicycle the right size."

Together they walked companionably back toward the house, Enoch pushing the bicycle, it's tires making a hushed crunching sound against the road. The fall air was cooling and she shivered in the rising breeze.

After a few moments of companionable silence, Kate found herself blurting out a question she'd been pondering even more since the previous Sunday sermon. "Enoch, have you ever seriously thought about leaving this life? Not living in the plain, Amish world?"

She swallowed hard, knowing it was a big question and a big topic, but she'd felt closer to him in the last few weeks than ever before. She felt she could talk to him again. Although she'd told him of her frustrations when they were courting years ago, he hadn't told her his thoughts at the time and they'd never talked about it afterwards. She'd always wondered.

"I thought about it." His words were brief, even clipped. He kept pushing the bicycle, not offering anything more.

She reached up to brush a flying insect away from her face. "We've...never talked about what happened when I went away."

The subject had lain between them—as had the topic of her marriage to Jakob—never discussed, but still present.

"No." He responded in that same clipped way.

"Are you...angry? Can we not talk about it?"

Enoch turned his head toward her as they entered the lane up to their house. "I don't see what good could come of that now."

She said nothing to this, daunted by both his tone and the wintery sound in his voice. Daunted and angry.

"We once could talk. About anything." Snatching at a high grass seed pod that had grown out over the lane, Kate tried to keep her voice level. Her mother had told her more could be gained with honey than vinegar. "I once even told you about my frustrations and questions about this life."

"Yes, you did. And yet after you came back from your *rumspringa*, you joined the church and married Jakob Bieler."

She heard the bitterness in his voice and wondered that she'd let herself believe he was over the issues between them. Enoch had married her. Here it was though. The wound had been opened and she couldn't seem to shut her hurt back inside her.

"You not only told me I had no right—as a girl—to go on *rumspringa*, you also never wrote me while I was away. Even though I wrote and begged you to respond. You turned your back on me." Kate stared ahead at the house they approached. They lived there together as man and wife, but all that lay open between them now left her feeling like he was that stranger again, that person she had never known. A man who'd hurt her so deeply she'd turned to Jakob Bieler's lukewarm love.

He stopped as they walked toward the house, turning to look at her. In deep sincere words, he said, "I was wrong not to respond. I'm sorry about that."

At the house steps now, Kate stared at him. He wasn't an arrogant, self-righteous man—those could even be found amongst the plain people—but she'd never before heard Enoch make such an open admission of being in the wrong. He'd...apologized to her. The fact startled her, even though she knew she was due an apology.

For several long moments, they stood gazing at one another, a humble expression on his face that left her feeling like a puddle inside. Through a clogged throat, she managed to say, "I missed you...terribly...when I was in Baltimore. And when you didn't write or respond to my letters, I felt as if a limb had been hacked off."

He looked down at the bicycle balanced in his grip between then. When he lifted his gaze to hers he said simply, "I'm sorry. I was...upset that you'd gone. It's not an excuse."

Not knowing how to respond, she said nothing as she turned and went up the porch steps.

"I'll put the bicycle in the barn," he said. "We can keep it there in the empty stall."

"Enoch," Kate said, her throat feeling tight, "you've...never...wondered about what it would be like? Not to live this life?"

He stood on the ground in front of the house, sloping away to the barn, her bicycle balanced in front of him. "No, Kate. I mean, yes. I thought about it—for maybe a day. And I went on *rumspringa* like other young men, but I love this life. It suits me to a tee."

Resting her trembling hand on the porch railing, she held his gaze. "And all those years ago, when I told you my questions— you never said anything about that. Or anything really. I thought you'd responded, but you didn't."

He stood below her, the rays of the descending winter sun burnishing his dark hatless, head, his plain white shirt outlining his muscled, sturdy form. "No, I didn't."

Stepping closer to the porch railing, she heard young Sarah's voice at the side gate, bidding goodbye to the school friend her daughter walked home with.

"Why?" Kate's words felt tight in her throat. "Why didn't you say anything to me about my doubts? Why did you not write to me in Baltimore?"

For a moment, she thought he wasn't going to respond even now, the sounds of Sarah tromping in the house's back door signaling a close to their time alone.

Enoch let the bicycle shift forward, as his gaze brooded on the field next to the barn. He looked back to her then. "Because. I know you hate what seems like the narrowness of the church's view of men and women. Things like that puppy, Aaron Yoder, spouted."

"Mamm! Mamm!" Sarah called to her.

"It doesn't have to be that black and white, Kate," he said, "that's all. It's not one or the other."

"Mamm!" Sarah's voice came through the front screened door.

"I'm putting this away," Enoch said, turning toward the barn. "I'll be in shortly."

A week later, Enoch's father, Samuel, dropped by the farm. "Enoch, my son! How are you?"

As they hugged, slapping one another affectionately on the back, he noted again that his father seemed thinner now, not the man of Enoch's youth.

"How are you, boy? Did you and Kate get the barn roof repaired?"

The two men started walking toward the house, Samuel's horse and buggy tied at a post near the barn. The winter air was crisp, the grass dry now and crunchy under their feet.

"Yes, I finally got that finished and we filled in around the barn's corner foundation pier. Those were some storms." They climbed the steps to the farm house porch.

"Yes, I thought my house might blow away. Such a strong storm! More like a spring blow. I would expect a winter snow at this season." Samuel took off his wide-brimmed hat.

"Kate!" Enoch called out as he opened the door, the smell of Kate's delicious breakfast still hanging in the air. "Come say hello to my father."

Coming across the kitchen as she dried her hands on a towel, Kate beamed at Enoch's father. "Samuel! I'm so glad you came by. Here, put your hat in this chair by the door. Isn't it early for you to be out? We just finished breakfast, although Enoch was out earlier to milk the cow. Come sit by the fire."

"Ah, *danke*, daughter." Enoch's father sank into the rocker closest to the glowing hearth.

"I've been out to see my old friend, Rachel—you remember John Hochstetler's mother?"

"Of course. Hannah's mother-in-law." Kate sat in the rocker next to Samuel as Enoch stopped to pat Sarah, where she sat scribbling away at the table.

"Nice picture," he murmured, looking over her shoulder at her drawing of old Bessie pulling the buggy.

"Enoch!" Samuel called out to his son. "You do remember Rachel's younger son, Joseph?"

Turning, Enoch said, "Yes, of course. Joseph and I were in school together. We sometimes help one another out when it's harvest time."

"Yes, well then you know that Joseph's young wife, Rebecca, just had a baby." The older man shook his head, the fire in the fireplace hissing and popping. "Rachel is very worried about her. The *Boppli* cries a lot and Rebecca's struggling. Rachel stays to help as much as she can—as does Rebecca's mother—but Rachel is getting older."

Samuel smiled before going on. "As are we all. Anyway, Rebecca's mother has young children of her own to care for. I believe several other women have stopped in, too, but Rebecca can hardly get any sleep with the *Boppli's* crying."

Kate made a face at his *Daed*. "Sarah cried a lot when she was a little *Boppli*. Jakob told me about it. Even when I married him—when she was five—she had crying spells."

"That must have been difficult." Enoch stared at her with a different picture of her early married years to Jakob. He hadn't wanted to think about it before, angry at her being happy with another man, but God was helping him forgive her. Maybe things hadn't been as rosy for the pair as he'd thought. Maybe they'd both been prideful and in the wrong.

"You were only a youngie yourself when you became Sarah's mam."

Kate laughed softly in deprecation. "I'm sure Rebecca will figure it out. I did fast enough. She's a good girl from everything I know about her."

"Yah," Samuel said, looking at her with narrowed eyes, "but you had your mam. She was a smart woman was Elizabeth. Rebecca has no one but Rachel and, at times, her own mother, who is also frazzled. It isn't good. Rebecca's husband, Joseph was also the youngest of his family, so he hasn't been around *Bopplis* either. Not much."

"But..." Enoch said slowly as he stood in front of his father and her at the fireplace, "you could help her, Kate. Rebecca might benefit from you're having dealt with, you know, everything you dealt with."

Samuel lifted his brows as he pondered the thought. "That might not be a bad idea, having a settled woman friend a little older than her. Kate's about her own age. Not like Rachel and Rebecca's *Mamm*. She might hear suggestions on how to make the baby easier coming from you."

"Oh, I don't think so," Kate disagreed, shaking her dark head. "The poor girl doesn't need someone else telling her what to do."

"No," Enoch said after a moment, "but you wouldn't do that. Would you?"

"That certainly wouldn't have helped me." Kate thought about it for a moment. "My mother just…helped. Took Sarah to her house to help her make soap. Took Sarah and me with her to the general store. She listened to me, to my fears… To Sarah who was missing her own *Mamm*, even though she didn't remember her much, she was so young when her mom died."

Silence fell, only broken by the popping of the fire and the scratch of Sarah's pencil on her paper.

Finally, Samuel said meditatively, "What Rebecca needs is a friend, more than another mother."

After another few minutes, Enoch said, "That's right. Your mom was more of a friend, wasn't she, Kate? And I could tell by the way you took care of the Hochstetler's baby at worship last time that you're comfortable with *Bopplis*, even little ones."

The more he thought about it, the more certain he was that Kate was just the person to show God's love to struggling Rebecca. "You could help out around the house. Maybe get Rebecca to take the *Boppli* in the buggy to the store. Sarah could drive Bessie. Even if the *Boppli* cries all the way, it would have to help her poor *Mamm* to get out of their house."

"I suppose so," she agreed, looking thoughtful, her expression sympathetic. "I had my *Mamm* and Hannah when I first married and was…you know…dealing with everything."

Looking at Kate now in her sweet concern for a girl she'd never been particular friends with, Enoch wanted to hug her close. She could be so kind.

"*Mamm*?" Sarah called from the table. "Come see if I spelled this right. I want to put Bessie's name right here."

"Of course, *Boppli*." She got up from the rocker next to Samuels, her skirt *shushing* as she went to look over Sarah's shoulder.

"Are you thinking about planting beans in that far field of yours?" Samuel asked after a moment.

As he was staring at his wife bending over Sarah's work, his father had to ask the question again. Enoch jerked his thoughts to the current moment. "I don't know yet. I'm considering several different crops."

He turned back toward the table. "Kate, I think you should be Rebecca's friend. I think you could help her learn to be a good mam...like your mom was to you. I think you'd be good at helping her."

She looked up from Sarah's work, flushing a little. "But Enoch, I've been thinking. She and I were never all that close. I don't want to make her feel worse by intruding at this moment. Besides, I'm...often less than the ideal Amish woman."

His gaze was fixed on her face. He knew what she was thinking, that her doubts about this life made her not the best to befriend the young mother. He thought they made her the perfect one. "I think you can do this well. She needs you. You wouldn't be likely to judge her—she'd know that. You'd be kind and generous at it. All that God asks us to be."

CHAPTER EIGHT

Two days later, Kate sat in a chair across from Rebecca Hochstetler. The main living area of the Hochstetler farm house felt stuffy and filled with stress. Her eighteen year-old hostess's hair was pulled off her face in a haphazard bun and she wore no *kapp*. Sitting on the old-fashioned settle, her shoulders drooping, she looked exhausted and overwhelmed like Enoch's *Daed* had said.

"Can I hold the *Boppli*?" Kate sent her a friendly smile.

"Of course." Rebecca sat on the sturdy ladder-backed bench, her newborn held in the crook of her arm. She shifted the bundle of fussy, irritable infant, handing him over to Kate. "He's...not always very happy."

Grimacing in a friendly manner at the young mother, she received the *Boppli* into her arms. "I know that can make it hard. Remember, your sister-in-law, Hannah, has four *Bopplis* and will soon deliver a fifth. We are good friends and I remember the early days of her becoming a mother weren't always smooth. She says everyone else seems to have always-happy *Bopplis,* while hers are often crabby."

"Hannah's a good woman." Watching her take the babe, Rebecca took a deep, tired breath. "She said she'll come over when she gets a moment. I know her child is due any day."

Kate stood with the squirming, red-faced *Boppli*, swaying with him in her arms. "Yes. I tell you what—why don't you do whatever you need to do—while I take care of little Isaiah. You may need to take a little nap. I can certainly understand if you do. I'll wake you if the baby needs you."

Rebecca looked hesitant.

"Or if you prefer," Kate smiled at her, remembering just how overwhelmed she'd felt when she assumed the mother role, "I'll wash the dishes and make supper while you look after Isaiah. I like cooking and I don't mind cleaning up. Maybe I could make you some soup for later."

"Mothers are always supposed to want to be with their babies." Rebecca spoke the sentence in a voice of misery.

Seeing the distress on the younger woman's face and adding that to the squalling infant in her arms, plus the dirty house, Kate's heart swelled. "Don't do that to yourself, Rebecca. This is a lot to handle. If you want help with the house, I'm glad to do it while you care for Isaiah, but it's not a sin to take a break from the baby. Take a nap! It doesn't mean you don't love him."

She'd often felt the same despair she saw now on Rebecca's face when she'd started raising a still-grieving Sarah when Kate had first married Jakob.

"I've prayed and prayed." The young mother's words burst out of her. "I must be a very sinful woman. Isaiah just won't stop crying!"

Shifting the fussing *Boppli* to her hip, Kate sat down next to Rebecca reaching over to cover the girl's clenched hand with her own. "Never think that. God loves us, Rebecca. Of course, this is a hard time. New babies are often irritable at first. Each of Hannah's were crabby, but it does get better."

The other girl sent her a smile that wavered. "Do you think so?"

"Of course." Looking around the disordered room, Kate found herself asking, "Where is Joseph?"

She knew criticizing her young friend's husband wouldn't help, but she couldn't help her own thoughts. Why wasn't he helping his wife more?

114

In a listless voice, Rebecca said, "Oh, he's at our neighbors, helping with some repairs from the recent storms. I think he's probably glad to get out of the house."

"Has he...has he not," Kate glanced at the messy kitchen, "not been able to help with the *Boppli*?"

"It isn't a man's work." Rebecca's mouth thinned as she clamped it shut. "His mother insists I can do this alone. She and my mother have both been here several times, but they always want to play with Isaiah and, when they do, I'm too tired to do anything around the house."

"I know I should." The words seemed to burst from her.

"His mother? Rachel Hochstetler?" Kate remembered this was the name Enoch's father had mentioned.

"Yes."

A bolt of anger went through her as Kate looked into the weary, angry, distressed face of the young mother in front of her. Even though Samuel would naturally want to help his neighbors, he seemed not to see that helping his overwhelmed wife was more important.

Rising to again sway with little Isaiah, Kate forced herself to smile. "Never mind, Rebecca. You nap now. My Sarah's in school and my house is fine. I'll take care of the *Boppli* now. Rest."

"Are you sure?" Even as she asked, longing gleamed on Rebecca's face.

"Yes, of course. I'm sure he'll sleep. If he needs feeding, I'll bring him to you."

With the new mother escaping into her bedroom to sleep, Rebecca went outside with the fussy infant. "Come on, Isaiah. We'll go look at the chickens in your *Daed's* pen."

Holding her cranky bundle face-out over her arm, she supported Isaiah's bottom as she walked down the shallow porch steps to the chicken pen.

She'd always hoped for children of her own. It had seemed as if having children would have drawn her closer to Jakob...and she'd always dreamed of caring for her own child. It hadn't happened, of course, and…she'd grown fearful over time that she was barren. The possibility still haunted her.

When at the pen that held the chickens, she swayed back and forth as they scratched at the earth with their soothing clucks. She thought about Rebecca's dilemma. She thought about Jakob's awkwardness in trying to comfort the still-grieving Sarah and she thought about the many women who thought they had to be perfect in God's eyes. There was something to be said for comforting those who didn't realize they were loved by God, even in their imperfect state.

She might not have borne a child of her own body, but she felt tremendous sympathy for the challenging job of mothering.

After a while, she realized Isaiah had fallen completely asleep, his small body sagging in oblivion. She went back into the house and placed the sleeping baby in a cradle there beside the fireplace. Then, she began quietly cleaning the kitchen. She first filled one half of the sink with sudsy water and washed every dirty dish she could find. After rinsing each one, she dried it and put it back into the cupboard as silently as she could. Both baby Isaiah and his mother needed to sleep undisturbed.

Just as quietly, she found a broom and began to clean the floor. The washing would wait until after she'd done theirs tomorrow.

"I don't know what's gotten into Rebecca Hochstetler," Elder Fisher said, pulling his mouth down in a disapproving frown at the meeting a week later. "I see she and the child aren't here. Women have been having *Bopplis* for years. It's nothing to make such a fuss about."

Kate stopped walking toward the kitchen, staring at the elder in disbelief. Services were over and clumps of people stood chattering in the living area of the Hochstetler home, waiting for seats to open around the lunch tables set out, as wonderful lunch smells wafted from the kitchen.

"And you, Kate Miller," the elder said to her, apparently catching sight of her standing there. "Didn't Samuel Miller tell me you'd gone to help her with the babe? I know several others went, as well. Did you not tell her to pray to God to forgive her for her unbelief? She should be grateful she's borne a healthy child."

At that moment surrounded by the men she'd grown up respecting for the most part, Kate wished the ground would swallow her. If only she'd gotten to the women in the kitchen before. As it was, all talk around them had stopped and everyone fell silent, listening to the elder's condemning words.

She felt the disapproval of Elder Fisher's gaze and wished for one moment she could hide in Enoch's strong arms. Not that she necessarily had the right to seek his comfort. Not fully even now.

Stiffening her backbone as she took steps toward the older man, Kate tried to reign in her frustration before she burst into the intemperate speech her mother had always warned her about. "Elder Fisher, Rebecca isn't struggling with an unbelief in God. She's overwhelmed with the demands of new motherhood to a very irritable child."

The elder frowned more as he responded. "We are the leaders for our children. Maybe Rebecca didn't want this child or the natural changes motherhood brings into a woman's life as all Godly women do. Why her own mother told Rachel Hochstetler that Rebecca was making this larger than it needed to be. The babe is fine, according to her."

Words erupted out of Kate as heat ran up her cheeks. "Elder Fisher, have you ever tried to quiet an inconsolable child? Held him as the day closes out and been unable to give him relief? Rebecca's *Boppli* cries with the colic and while Rachel and Rebecca's mother may drop by her home once in a while, Rebecca and Joseph are the ones dealing with him."

Under a tree ten feet away where he'd been visiting with a neighbor, Enoch's attention was drawn suddenly by the angry, tense tone of his wife's lifted voice. She stood in front of Elder Fisher, her unsmiling face not at all respectful, her eyes stormy.

Without realizing it, he found himself taking several steps toward Kate, drawn toward the situation as if he could somehow diffuse it.

"Well, who else would deal with her child, but Rebecca?" Elder Fisher's eyes narrowed. "Perhaps, Kate Miller, Rebecca needs to listen to older, wiser heads...such as her mother and Rachel. And even her elders. She doesn't need to be told to coddle her son, as it seems you are doing. Have you told her to drop to her knees to pray for God's forgiveness for any sin that may have brought on her distress?"

Enoch saw the rigidity in Kate's body, saw the sudden lift of her chin. Without hesitation, he took another step forward, saying. "Elder Fisher, Kate has helped Rebecca and Joseph immensely. She's been at their home nearly every day this week, not a hindrance, but a help. Joseph himself came by the house only yesterday to tell me what a blessing she's been to them, how much more rested and calm Rebecca has been since Kate's been coming over."

The elder turned his stern, disapproving gaze to Enoch. "That is as it may be, son, but you should have better authority over your wife, Enoch, that she not speak so disrespectfully to those who know better."

"I haven't heard her speak disrespectfully to you just now or to Rebecca's mother or mother-in-law. To my knowledge, she's not said a bad word against anyone. And she's right about the *Boppli*. I was at Rebecca and Joseph's home last evening when the child cried long and hard."

The elder regarded him stonily.

"I'd certainly want some help if I had a child like theirs." Enoch shifted, bracing his feet apart a little as he faced the man. "She's fine, Kate is...and she's right. They did need help. We need to accept God's helpers, however these are presented to us."

Beside him, Kate took a deep breath, letting it out as if she'd run a long race. In that moment, Enoch knew that she'd had a point all along. God was too big to speak only through the voices of often-narrow men.

Later, riding back to their farm alone in the buggy with Enoch since young Sarah had begged to spend the night with a friend, Kate sat next to him, feeling overwhelmed by his standing up for her. She huddled her coat around her, the air December cool, tucking her hands into her armpits.

Enoch gripped the reins with strong, bare fingers, apparently impervious to the cold. She wanted to tell him how much his speech had meant to her, but she wasn't sure how to form the words. One stood up to bullies, but it seemed wrong to classify a church leader this way.

He guided the buggy without speaking, old Bessie clip-clopping along, the silence between them filled with the sound of her hooves. The woods and fields around them were barren in the pale, watery winter light. When the weather warmed with the spring, they'd be a rich green and pungent with milk thistle that grew wild in this area.

If she had to guess, she'd think they would have snow soon, the air had grown that crisp. It smelled cold.

"Kate," Enoch said suddenly, turning his head to look over at her, "I've never...never asked you about your time in Baltimore with your uncle."

Jarred out of her thoughts, she shot him a startled look. The subject of that period had seemed off limits between them...like her marriage to Jakob.

Enoch had strongly disapproved of her having time in Baltimore, angry that she'd gone against his wishes. Little did she know that by going on *rumspringa*, she'd apparently stepped outside his heart.

"No," she faltered a little in her response, not knowing what to say. "You haven't...you never mentioned it."

"What was it like? What was your time in the *Englischer* world like?" His dark hat shifted back on his head, he looked over at her. "Tell me. I truly want to know."

As she hesitated, completely thrown by his bringing up the subject, he cleared his throat. "I know I never wrote to you. I..."

His words trailed off.

"It was..." She struggled to form her thoughts. "It was...lonely. Mostly."

He looked over at her, their gazes holding for a long moment, only the sound of Bessie's steps between them.

"You never...you never wrote." She looked at her hands, gripping the sleeves of her coat shut. "I...wrote you."

"Yes, I know." Without offering any explanation, he said, "Tell me what you thought of that world. You came back to this one."

"*Ya.*" She stuck her hands into her armpits again. "I don't know. It was noisy... Busy. What did you think of it, from your time in the *Englischer* world? You went on a *rumspringa.*"

"Yes, although not to that city."

Seeming to find the back of the horse fascinating, he brooded on Bessie. "It was, I don't know, exciting, I guess. And noisy, like you said. I went to stay with my cousins who had rented a place for several months. I liked television. At least, parts of it. I worked there for a friend of my cousin."

"Yes, my uncle had a big television and then several smaller ones in all the rooms." She didn't know what to add to this. She'd been so consumed with him not writing her, wondering each day when the post would run, that she hadn't cared much about the strange world around her. Her determination to go on *rumspringa* was more about the restrictions placed on women in her world than on any desire to leave that world.

Then, of course, she'd been hurt and gotten angry with him for ignoring her and her letters.

"There were men all around in that town," Enoch said heavily, "going out with girls... Talking badly about those girls."

Kate said nothing, not sure where the conversation was going.

"Was your uncle nice to you?" Turning to look at her again, Enoch seemed as if he wanted to know.

"Yes, I suppose. Yes. He'd grown up with my mother, of course, and he told me of her before she left the *Englischers* and married my father. He talked of my mother." She smiled as the memories washed over her. "Of my mother going to college, of the messes she got into and of her college degree."

120

"The men she courted before your *Daed*?" His voice hardened a little.

"I guess. Some. Uncle Brandon was very kind. He tried to make my time there as good as it could be."

The clip clop of Bessie's hooves again was the only sound.

"They had big buildings in Baltimore," she offered. "And Uncle Brandon took me to see Washington, D.C. It's very large and has lots of beautiful city places—buildings and parks."

"Did—does—your uncle have a wife?"

"He had a girlfriend. Her name was Jennifer and she worked in a library. I think…" Kate squinted as she tried to dredge up information she'd only partly attended to, at the time. "I think she had a son in college. I don't know where. I never met him."

Kate shivered as a gust of wind swept over them.

"You're cold," Enoch said. "There's another lap blanket in the back. Put it over your lap."

"Oh-Okay." She turned, stretching to reach into the back seat, pulling out a lap blanket finally. Smoothing it over her lap with gratitude, she buried her hands beneath the thick fabric.

"Are you warm enough now? Would you like my coat around your shoulders?"

"Oh, no!" She threw him a startled look. "You'd freeze without it."

The corner of Enoch's mouth lifted. "Nah. I'm wearing a thick shirt and I have an undershirt, too. I'm fine."

She liked the sound of his voice when he smiled. It was gentler somehow. Kate smiled back at him. "You keep the coat, anyway. I'm fine now."

Shifting his gaze back to the road, Enoch clucked at the horse pulling the buggy. "Get up, Bessie."

Letting the warmth of the lab blanket seep into her, Kate sat beside him contentedly, the chill air of the season prickling at her nose.

After a minute, he looked over. "So in the whole time you were with your uncle, you never met this Jennifer's son…or any other young men. I'm surprised. It seemed like the ways of the

Englischer world was that the young men always noticed and pursued attractive women."

"I don't know. I never met the son and...I wasn't in Baltimore to find another boy." She didn't say it, but the only boy she'd thought about back then was him. Enoch and how she'd love him and how he'd...dumped her for having a mind of her own and going on *rumspringa*. Even when he told her she had no right.

Kate fell silent. Enoch was wrong to demand she not go to Baltimore, but her pain and disappointment had hardened her heart and... Led her into making choices she shouldn't have. She'd been so angry and so hurt that she'd stopped praying and had rashly taken matters into her own hands, not thinking to let God sort it out.

Instead, she come back from Baltimore and married the first man who asked her. And the match had only brought her sadness and distress, other than Sarah. She'd mourned Jakob's sudden death, but not as a wife should. There was no admitting to it, but she'd often felt annoyed with her husband and his inability to get things done. His overall ineptitude at being a father.

She'd cried for him though, because Jakob was a son of God and hadn't deserved to die.

"Enoch."

He turned to look at her.

"I want to thank you for what you said to Elder Fisher. No," she said as he made a dismissive gesture. "It was...truly wonderful, to have you speak up for me and for Rebecca."

"The elder was wrong, that's all." Enoch shrugged, looking back at the road. "You have made a difference in befriending her, Kate. And you were right in what you said to the Elder. I don't think the *Boppli* cried because of Rebecca having sinned."

She saw the corner of his mouth lift as he spoke again, "More like the *Boppli* took one look around at this hard life and the world man has wrought and started crying at the sight of us."

Chuckling at this, she took her now-warm hand and slipped it into his. Enoch turned back to look at her with a full smile before he turned back to the horse.

Dear Lord, Kate prayed silently as she lay next to Enoch that night, *thank You for Enoch.* The quilts pulled up under her chin, she huddled in the warm cocoon. The December wind howled around the corners of the house as a tear leaked from the corner of her eye. She knew God hadn't sent her the trials of the last year. Some of them she'd chosen—like the sad marriage to Jakob—and some had come in the random nature of this hard life.

But she had no doubt that the husband beside her, as infuriating as he could sometimes be, was God's gift to her, to help her grow and to shelter her.

"Kate! Kate!"

Looking up from her sudsy kitchen floor ten days later, she saw Rebecca through her screen door. "Come in," Kate called, the warm, steamy smell of wash water rising from the wet floor. "I'm here! On the floor behind the table."

Hearing the screen door slam, she craned her neck to look around the table. Rebecca, carrying a swaddled Isaiah, walked over.

With her cheeks pink from the winter chill and the prayer *kapp* on her head looking freshly-laundered, the new mother looked very different than when Kate first offered help.

"You got out of the house!" Kate smiled up at her. "That's great."

Rebecca beamed at her. "Yes, and Isaiah's now sleeping up to six hours at a time. I can finally get a little rest myself."

"I told you it would get better—not that I've borne babies myself, but Hannah's *Bopplis* all got more regular after a few weeks. Did he cry last evening, like the other nights?"

Making a face, the younger woman sat on a chair several feet from the damp kitchen floor where she could converse with Kate, gently settling the sleeping bundle onto her lap and loosening his blanket. "Yes, of course. It's so hard not to be able to comfort him. He just cries and cries until he finally goes to sleep."

Kate returned to scrubbing at the floor planks, rinsing her scrub cloth in the bucket of cooling water. "I know. I remember

Hannah talking about envying other mothers with *Bopplis* that slept peacefully at meetings, the women looking well rested and tidy."

"Yes!" Rebecca smiled ruefully. "I don't think I've ever envied so much before. Isaiah and I went to the general store yesterday with Joseph and the other little *Bopplis* there with their mothers were sleeping like angels. Not Isaiah, though. He just kept fussing."

Having dried her hand on her apron, Kate reached over to gently touch the blanket around the *Boppli*. She kept her voice lowered. "He's sleeping well now, though."

Rebecca smiled at the infant on her lap. "He is, thankfully, although this may be the only nap he gets today."

"Hopefully not." Kate straightened, plunging her cloth back into the water and wringing it out. "Little *Bopplis* need their sleep."

"Listen, Kate. I stopped by to give you my mother's thank you. She came by the house and we talked. She saw how much," Rebecca dipped her head, "better we're doing, Isaiah and I, and when I told her you've been coming over a lot to help, she— well—she got quiet. I think she realizes she could have helped more."

Kate didn't say anything, not wanting to sound critical.

"Anyway," Rebecca beamed at her, "*Mamm* wanted me to pass on her thanks. She said you've been a good friend—and it's helping her see how she can be a better grandmother. She said she wants to tell you that herself when she sees you at the next service."

"I'll be glad to talk with your *Mamm*. I haven't seen her the last few church meetings." She smiled, feeling a flush of pleasure at the compliment. In this way, at least, she could feel she was working in God's service.

CHAPTER NINE

Pushing his wood plane along the surface of the piece that would form the fourth leg of Sarah's new bed, Enoch paused to run his hand over the surface. Despite the January chill outside of the barn, he'd thrown off his coat and rolled up his shirt sleeves. The work and the combined heat from the horses in their stalls kept him warm.

He'd been right that Kate's generous heart would go out to the struggling Rebecca Hochstetler. The young mother had needed her and Kate had reached out to help. With her warm heart and good sense, she'd immediately pitched in to help the girl.

She belonged here with him, in this life. He'd been right to keep her uncle's letter from her…not that she'd see it if she knew.

He recognized the likelihood of her not forgiving him, if she ever found out the truth, but the only way he saw that happening would involve her trying again to contact her mother's brother. He didn't think she would, but that possibility kept Enoch awake, staring up into the darkness with her warmth beside him in bed. Of course, if she ever found her uncle had responded to her plea with an offer of assistance, Enoch figured he could lie and say the letter had gone astray.

But truth was God's way.

A frustrated sigh gusted out of Enoch just as the scrape of the barn door opening could be heard behind him.

"What are you doing out here?" Kate closed the barn door against the January chill, huddling a jacket around herself.

"Nothing." Enoch continued smoothing the piece of wood in the vise, his muscles bunching under his shirt as he drew back to push the plane forward across the wood.

She wandered over past the stalls and hoisted herself onto the tailgate of the farm wagon, next to where he worked. "Looks like a lot of effort for nothing."

Not stopping his work, he shot her a look, the corner of his mouth lifting. Smart-mouthed, ornery woman. Beautiful with her dark hair tucked under her prayer *kapp* and her blue eyes sparkling at him. Was it wrong to pray she never discovered his deceit? He believed God wanted her here, married to Enoch, but in the Bible, Sarah had also thought she needed to help God along by arranging for Abraham to sleep with her handmaiden. That hadn't worked out so well.

Enoch again ran a hand over the wood, checking for splinters.

Still watching him from the wagon tailgate, her feet swinging like a little girl, Kate asked, "What are you making?"

He knew he was only quibbling, trying to find a solace for his guilt, but she'd appeared happier in the last two months. Kate no longer seem to be drowning in the loss of her parents as she had when she'd come to propose marriage to him.

"Why do you think I'm making anything?" he said it in a teasing, provocative voice. She brought out the worst and best in him.

"I can see you're building something. Let's see… What do we need in the house? Maybe I can guess."

Her response was playful, too, and he had the urge to kiss her, but that could lead to a place they didn't have time for. Enoch couldn't help smiling at the thought.

The push of his plane shushed against the wood he worked on, narrowing one end of the bed foot in a graceful way. The other smoothed pieces of wood on the work bench behind him had been narrowed in the same way. Several larger pieces of wood sat off to the side, their sides turned away. The scent of freshly-shaved wood filled that part of the barn, mingling with the smell of the animals.

"Another chair for when we host church gatherings?"

"Woman," he stopped his work to wipe at his damp brow, "do you not have something else to do besides bother me?"

His words were accompanied by the same teasing smile because he was glad she'd come to the barn.

"No. The house is clean and our supper stew is already bubbling on the stove. I have a few minutes to pester you before Sarah gets here. Then I'll have to go in to work with her on her schooling, but not yet."

He loosened the vise screw and took out the planed board, placing it next to the other three with an economy of movement. "Then I guess I'll have to let you in on my secret."

"Yea!" Kate wiggled in anticipation. "Sounds like fun."

He gave a snort. "Sometimes you seem like you're no older than your daughter."

Giggling, she didn't bother to deny this.

"If you must know, I'm building a new bed for Sarah." He moved over to shift the larger piece of wood around so she could see the front.

"Sarah has a bed," she said in a startled voice as the full glory of the headboard dawned on her. "But not like this. Oh, Enoch."

She hopped off the wagon and walked forward to trace the carved roses at the top of the unfinished headboard. "Oh, my. Oh, Enoch."

"What? Isaac helped me start. He's the real furniture-maker." He frowned at her. He hadn't thought Sarah's new bed would make Kate unhappy. "Are you crying? Why are you crying? She needs a bigger bed."

Kate clutched the raw wood headboard to herself, tears leaking out the corners of her eyes. She exclaimed in a hushed tone, "It's beautiful! Oh, Enoch, she'll love it."

"I hope so. I thought she'd like it. She's a good girl. I should have the whole thing finished in a few more days with the cold weather keeping me indoors." He put the plane back into its place on the work bench. "Her old bed is rickety, having been a hand-me-down from my *Daed's* house."

"This is the kindest, sweetest thing." She sniffled as she pulled the headboard forward as if giving the wood a hug. Turning then, she hugged Enoch fiercely. "Sarah will love it. It's simple and plain, but has just those few field roses on it."

He felt his heart contract in his chest, flushing a little. "You're not crying again, are you? 'Cause I can burn this."

Whipping around after she'd gently leaned the headboard against the barn wall, she said, "Don't you dare!"

He sent her a crinkled smile that faded away. "I won't. I'm teasing."

He went back to the wood he'd smoothed, somberly loosening the vise. At least he could absolve himself in one way. "I've been doing a lot of thinking, Kate."

Hoisting herself on the wagon again, she said, "You have? About what?"

Enoch looked at her. "Us. About those early courting days."

"Oh."

"You were—" he broke off to clear his voice. "You were right, Kate. I wasn't being fair in not wanting you to go to Baltimore."

She drew a deep breath, letting it out as she frowned at him, her dangling feet no longer swinging.

Moving over to pull the smaller board off the wall, he said, "I was afraid, Katie. I realize that now."

Kate stared at him, her eyes narrowing as if she couldn't make sense of what he'd said. "Afraid? You? What of?"

Enoch settled the footboard on his work bench, turning to look at her more fully. "That you wouldn't come back. You forget, Kate, that I'd been on *rumspringa* already—"

Her interruption was swift. "I knew that. That was part of what made your decree so frustrating. You were to go, but not me? And why wouldn't I come back?"

Shifting the footboard on to the work bench, he paused. "Like I said, I'd been out in the *Englischer* world. I knew...what it was like."

"And I didn't deserve the right to see it for myself?" She sounded frustrated.

This was what he hadn't wanted, why he hadn't talked about this with her before. "It wasn't that you didn't deserve it, Katie...."

She stared at him, waiting for him to go on with the words that had burst out of him.

Enoch took another breath, saying again, "It wasn't that you didn't deserve it."

He cleared his throat, running his hand absently over the wood in front of him. "I never told you much about my *rumspringa,* did I?"

"No, not much beyond saying that you and a cousin from another town rented a place to stay for a month."

"It was a room, Kate. I didn't have any non-Amish relatives. We rented single, shabby room together and my cousin found us jobs as bus boys in a cheap restaurant."

She said nothing, just looking at him with irritation still on her beautiful face.

He put his tools back down on the work bench. "I saw the *Englischer* men that came to that restaurant. How they wooed woman. I overheard them talking, in the eating area and in the restroom. They talked about 'getting laid' and promising women anything to get 'into their pants'."

Kate still looked at him, although he couldn't interpret her expression now.

"These were nice-looking men," Enoch said in frustration. "They looked like they could afford more than a shared room and they flattered and complimented these women."

"And you imagined me in their place," she concluded with a frown. "As if I would be like those deluded women?"

Leaning forward a little in his intensity, Enoch said, "You are so much more beautiful than most...so, so much. I knew the *Englischer* men would see that and want you."

"Maybe, but you should have told me. I deserved to—" She broke off what she'd started to say, a streak of some unreadable emotion crossing her normally-readable face. "You could have told me, but we both made mistakes. Back then."

Enoch didn't say anything, filled with sadness at his part in making the breach between them back then.

"I—" She scooted forward and jumped off the wagon to stand looking at him. "I didn't handle any of it the right way. I did just what my mother always cautioned me not to do. I let my heart—my hurt, stupid heart—lead me into…actions I shouldn't have made. I should have prayed more. Asked for God's guidance and taken no steps until I got His direction."

A hand on the work bench, he looked at her, not clear on what she meant.

Kate pushed away from the wagon, taking several steps toward the stalls before swinging back to look at him. "I should have come back from Baltimore and…and told you how angry I was that you hadn't responded. I should have yelled and hollered and…and beat on you."

Smiling at the image she described, he wished, too, she'd done that.

"…anything, but what I did." She gulped in air. "Anything but marry Jakob."

Like a plunk, her words fell into the silence between them.

Enoch's chest felt tight and his feet rooted to the wooden barn floor. They never talked of her earlier marriage.

Her back now to the farm wagon, she looked at him, her blue eyes troubled and her mouth trembling a little. "I shouldn't have married Jakob, Enoch. It…wasn't happy."

Not knowing what to say, he registered a shameful flush of exultation. She hadn't been happy with the man she married instead of Enoch. He knew it was wrong to wish unhappiness on another human being, but right now, he couldn't imagine more wonderful news.

Forcing himself not to mention that, he said honestly, "I'm sorry you weren't happy."

They stared at one another, the fact of tremendous unspoken things finally being spoken filling the space between them. All of the sudden, he knew that he'd not married her to get revenge, not hoped for her to be swallowed in regret. He wanted Kate to be filled with joy—at least as much as could be found on this earth.

Full honesty required him to say, "I hated your being married to Jakob, but I want you to be able to tell me about it. I want you to be able to tell me anything. Even beat on me, if you feel you must."

That surprised a spurt of laughter out of her and she said in a besotted voice, "Stupid."

"Tell me…about how it was for you." Hearing of her being another man's wife would be hard, but he knew with surety that her speaking to him of her first marriage would bring the closeness he wanted with her. It was as if God had inserted the realization into him.

With a deep sigh, Kate hoisted herself again on to the wagon. Hoping to encourage her to speak, Enoch returned to his work at the bench, shifting Sarah's new footboard so he could attach the legs.

"Um, okay. I-I don't think Jakob was a bad man. He didn't hurt me or treat me badly."

"I'm glad." Starting to work what would be the leg joint, he looked up at her so she'd know he was giving attention to what she said.

"I don't want to talk ill of the dead." She seemed to ponder. "Jakob just wasn't very good at—at taking care of Sarah and me. I probably shouldn't even say any of this…"

"Why not? You're not condemning Jakob. Just tell me how it was for you."

"We could hardly afford food." The words slipped out of her. "I—I sometimes sold things to get food for Sarah."

The fact that Jakob wasn't a particularly good farmer was well known and didn't surprise him, but he hadn't realized things were quite so bad. "Wait a minute, he had a farm. He raised crops and kept animals. Surely that kept you fed."

She shrugged. "I couldn't eat them because the farm animals—such as we had—and the crop yields were Jakob's only hope at building the farm. He had to sell anything he produced in order to get more seed and the other things he needed to keep the farm going."

Enoch didn't respond right away. It had been common knowledge that the farm land Jakob Beiler used was family land. "And when he was gone, the family used the crops to feed *Mamm* and *Daed* Beiler."

"Yes, that's why Sarah and I moved in with my parents." She drew in a deep breath before saying, "I married Jakob because I was so angry when I got back from Baltimore. You said nothing to me, as if we didn't know one another. I only saw you that once at church after my trip to stay with Uncle Brandon."

"I was still angry," he murmured, remembering it well. "Relieved you'd come back, but angry. You know how parents want to thrash their *younglies* when they feared for them?"

Kate nodded. "I was angry, too. That's why when Jakob came courting…, I didn't turn him away."

Still sitting on the wagon, she shook her head. "I was wrong, Enoch. I acted out of anger and that isn't God's way. Despite my mother telling me my whole life not to let my heart always lead me, I acted out of my anger. And we both suffered."

Seeing her there, bathed in remorse made Enoch's chest ache. "It wasn't only you that put all this in action, Kate. I told you, I was scared and angry myself. I should have written you back. It was cowardly of me not to."

"Oh, Enoch. We've been such fools." She looked at him, her face filled with regret…and love.

Dropping the chisel on his work bench, he walked slowly to where she sat on the wagon. He cupped her face in his hands as he moved in closer to her, registering the smoothness of her jaw and feeling the quick hitch as she drew in a breath. "You are mine now."

"Where shall I put the potatoes?" Rebecca Hostetler asked Kate three days later, as the Miller home buzzed with people who'd come to the church services she and Enoch were hosting. The smell of roasting meat and all kinds of delicious food filled the house.

"Anywhere, Becca. I've served up three more bowls. Just space them out." She turned aside, taking a basket of rolls from Hannah who jiggled new baby James in one arm as he fussed. "Go feed little James. We'll do this."

"*Danke,*" Hannah said with a smile, surrendering the basket and shifting the baby to her shoulder. "It won't take long. James suckles quickly."

"Take your time. Relax a little," Kate called after her.

At that moment, Enoch and one of the older boys of the congregation came past, carrying another long table. He looked her way, sending her a simmering, conspiratorial glance that made her blush from more than the heat of the stove. As they moved past with their heavy burden, she lowered her gaze and tried to calm her pulse.

"I'm taking these two bowls, Kate," Rebecca said from beside her. "I don't think I should try to juggle all three. I'll come back for the other one."

"Smart girl." Kate sent the younger woman a smile over her shoulder as she continued serving. "Is Isaiah still sleeping?"

"Yes." Rebecca picked up another bowl of potatoes, gesturing with her head toward the cradle in a warm corner of the living area. "All these bodies must be keeping him warm, but you'd think the chatter would wake him!"

Kate chuckled, "Ah, the blessings after your trials."

Hannah's new child and Rebecca's little Isaiah stirred Kate's desire for another child in their family. She prayed God would soon bless her and Enoch with a *Boppli* of their own. She'd not had the joy of giving birth when married to Jakob and it seemed fitting to hope that she could share this tremendous moment with Enoch.

Around them, the living area buzzed with the chatter of visiting neighbors and relatives, the windows steamed with the warmth from the gathering and the wood stove in the corner.

"Hey, Sarah sweetie," she called out to her young daughter as the girl slipped through the chattering throng. "Is Enoch through carrying in the tables? I can't see him."

"Yes," Sarah hugged her around the hips. "I think he's putting some places into the other rooms for people to eat."

Putting a caressing hand on the head of little blonde hugging her, the small prayer *kapp* perched on the back of Sarah's head, Kate handed her daughter a bowl of yeasty rolls. "Pass these out, honey, and we'll make you up a plate when you get back."

The next hour was filled with cooking and serving the church gathering as the hungry cycled through. A cheerful group of seven or eight women helped, some doing dishes and others putting food in serving bowls as it was needed. Kate had always enjoyed their hostings, even when growing up with her *Mamm* and *Daed*. It was a happy time of friends and family all sitting together.

It was a satisfaction to Kate that Elder Fisher had greeted her with marked respect when he first came to the gathering that morning. She knew his changed attitude was probably partly due to Rebecca's church service attendance, but Enoch's standing up for Kate couldn't have gone unnoticed.

Even if females weren't allowed to take roles of leadership in the church, she could see there were respected roles open to them.

The noise of the chattering community gathering got boisterous as the day wore on and the *youngies* ran through, slamming the door as they came in and out of the house.

It wasn't until Kate heard her name called twice that she registered the fact. Mr. Nilson, over on the other side of the room, was calling to her.

He stood by the door next to a man who's face was…familiar. The man's red nose made it clear that he'd just come in from the cold outside, as did his heavy jacket and cap. Paused in the act of taking another roasted chicken from the gaping gas oven, Kate felt herself turning to stone.

It was Uncle Brandon. Although her *rumspringa* in Baltimore had taken place over a sultry July and she'd never seen her uncle bundled up, she knew it was him. Kate had only met her mother's brother once before that visit, when she was eight years old and Elizabeth Lehman's only sibling had paid a visit to their little Pennsylvania town. At first, living with him in his Baltimore apartment had felt strange, but soon her misery over Enoch's silence had eclipsed everything else. Uncle Brandon had been kind, though. All through her blind grief and growing anger.

She'd recognize him anywhere.

Dropping the roasted chicken on to a platter on the stove, she quickly let the oven door bang shut as she turned to make her way through the tables with a broad, welcoming smile.

He stood by the door, looking very self-conscious. As Kate came up to him, she wiped her damp hands on her apron before extending them both to the man her mother had grown up beside. As she walked toward her relative, she vaguely registered Enoch approaching from her right.

"Uncle Brandon! Oh, how wonderful it is to see you!"

Three feet away from her, Enoch froze, his brain shutting down. Every muscle in his body seemed to lock up and he furiously scrambled to think of what to do to avoid the calamity before him. She would know; she would find out—that he'd lied, that he'd withheld her uncle's letter from her.

He could feel his heart thundering in his chest, but his mind was a blank. In his daze, he watched Kate move forward to hug her uncle, watched her smile and gesture both he and Sarah forward. Enoch knew he could lie, but he didn't think he could do it convincingly. She'd take one look at his face and know.

They were talking, her uncle's lips were moving. Around them, people moved and chattered and the whole scene took on the feeling of a nightmare for Enoch. As a boy, he'd once snatched a cooling tartlet from his mother's kitchen, wolfing it down in several bites and feeling sick afterwards. Sick with unchewed tartlet and sick with guilt.

The same sinking hole was in his midsection now, the same nausea. Only worse.

Flooded with apprehension, he watched Kate turn and scan the gathering of friends, spotting him standing there. She gestured him forward again, but he felt rooted to the floor as if he were a stuffed animal with no capacity to move. As though his ears had developed a crazed magnified hearing, he heard her uncle—his hat now clutched in his hands—offering condolences to Kate for the loss of her parents. Elizabeth, her mother. He talked of his shock that his only sister was no longer in this world.

And then the words that Enoch feared most came out of the uncle's mouth. It was as if by watching the man's mouth, the words revealing Enoch's deceit were clear before his vision. All in terrifying slowed motion.

"Didn't you get my letter? I wrote back. I never heard from you again and came to see if you still need help."

As he stood rooted to the living room floor, the voices around him grew louder, echoing the pounding of his heart, and took on a distorted, deafening tone. A roaring around him.

It flashed through his mind that he could lie, he could run, he could deny everything.

Kate stood next to her uncle, half-turned toward him, her hand on Sarah's shoulder. Confusion growing on her beautiful face, her dark hair smooth under her *kapp*. From feet away, Enoch saw her flash him a questioning glance. Saw her lean forward to hear better what her uncle said.

Almost without his conscious choice, Enoch moved forward, his steps carrying him into his darkest nightmare… But he couldn't run. He couldn't lie. At that moment, he knew he'd not be able to respect himself at all if he didn't own up to this.

Maybe, if God was with him, he'd get through this. Somehow. Keep Kate. Somehow. Enoch had never prayed so hard in his life. He kept taking slow steps toward the group by the door.

"…I was out of state on work," her uncle was saying, "and I'd had my mail held. When I got back—and read your letter about

Elizabeth and your father dying in that buggy accident—and you needing a home for yourself and the child..."

Enoch stopped beside Kate, drawing a ragged breath into his tight chest.

"...and then when you never answered the letter I sent—I'd have come right then myself to get you, but I couldn't get the time off work. We're in the middle of this huge contract. So, I sent you the letter, inviting you both to come to live with me, if only until you sorted everything out."

"But...I never got a letter." She spoke slowly, her brow knitted, her hands still resting on Sarah's shoulders. "I'd moved. Out of my parents' house. I wasn't at the same address—"

Kate glanced at Enoch, her words stopping. When she spoke again, her gaze stayed on his face, her speech slow and filled with conclusions. "—but this is a small town. The post office knew I'd moved. I told them I'd moved, changed my address. I gave them my new address...and name."

Turned fully now to face him, she stood next to her uncle and Enoch knew she'd figured it out. The truth was probably written on his face. Why? Why had he done it? Kate had already married him, already pledged to combine her life with his.

"You." Her eyes bored into his. "You got my letter. Didn't you? And kept it from me?"

The time for lying was over, Enoch knew, but he couldn't help saying with a shade of defensiveness, "You were my wife, Kate. My wife. We were married when the letter came. Was I supposed to let you leave?"

The part of the room where they stood fell quiet, as if everyone was listening to the moment. Uncle Brandon said nothing, his face anxious and still a little confused.

"So you decided? You didn't give me any choice. You took my mail and kept it from me."

Enoch couldn't deny her accusation. Clearing his throat, he stood before her, not trying to justify his actions. He'd destroyed the letter rather than let her know she didn't have to rely only on him, but he couldn't say this now. It had been a wrong action and nothing he could say would erase that.

"You—better than anyone, Enoch—you know my frustration with not getting to choose my own life. Yet you kept this choice from me."

He wanted to shout at her, to yell about his risk, about his having taken her and his enemy's child in, but he kept his jaw locked, his heart tangling with his head. Talking of his anger, of her part in everything would only make matters worse. This was no moment to fight and argue.

Sarah's face already held an apprehensive look, her brown eyes wide. He didn't want to scare the child any more, didn't want her to witness his own and her mother's unraveling...here in front of the community.

Glaring at him with hard blue eyes, Kate said, "Uncle Brandon, can Sarah and I...? I think maybe we should go back to Baltimore with you."

CHAPTER TEN

"I don't know what to do, Hannah." Kate sat at her friend's table hours later, both kept warm in the evening chill by their voluminous flannel nightgowns. A low fire still crackled in the shadowed room, the occasional popping of the burning wood the only sound in the room other than their hushed voices.

Capable hands wrapped around a mug of tea, her friend said, "I can hardly believe it of Enoch. He's always been such a true man. Always honest and fair. It's very puzzling. I don't think I'd have believed it of him, if he hadn't admitted himself that he destroyed the letter from your uncle."

"I know." The cup of tea bracket between her hands steaming gently, Kate reached up to rub a hand over her eyes. "I'm so grateful you and John invited Sarah and I to stay here tonight. I'm just so— I couldn't stay with Enoch."

A sob broke out of her and she clamped her hand to stifle the sounds as her shoulders shook with the grief shaking her body.

"Hush, now. Hush." Hannah left her seat to come hug Kate to her. "You and the child are always welcome here. Why, you know John and I invited you to move here after your parents' deaths."

Choking back her useless tears, Kate nodded. "I know. I know, but your home is already bursting at the seams, Hannah."

Her friend sat next to her, patting her shoulder as she wept into her hands.

Raising her ravaged face, Kate said, "It's just so complicated. I've felt drawn to Enoch for so long. I'm ashamed to admit this,

Hannah, but I never stopped feeling it, even though I married Jacob."

"I know," her friend said with a sad smile. "You didn't talk about it, but I knew you weren't happy with Jakob."

"I tried! I made sure I was a good wife to him and a loving mother to Sarah—well, I do love Sarah."

A new wave of tears spilled down her cheeks. "I was so angry with Enoch. For so long, I was angry." She lifted her head to admit. "I wouldn't have been so angry, I think, if I hadn't still felt a lot for him. Even when I tried to be the best wife I could be to Jakob."

"Probably not."

Kate made a growling sound. "How could Enoch do this? How could he so clearly deceive and lie to me?"

"I do see why you're so angry, but..."

Glaring at Hannah in the seat next to her, she demanded, "But? But what?"

"But by the time your uncle's letter arrived, you and Enoch were already married." The older woman grimaced. "You know we believe marriage is for life. What was Enoch to do?"

"He was to have been honest with me!" Kate said with venom. "At least, to have been honest with me."

"What would you have done?"

"I don't know." She shifted around in her seat. "I love this life. I do. I was raised in the church and I can't really see myself living in the *Englisch* world, but I have frustrations... I have questions about some things in the Ordnung."

Hannah nodded. "*Ya*, you have mentioned it—just barely, just enough for me to have guessed—"

Sniffing back her tears with indignation, Kate said, "Well, I talked to him about it, Hannah. All about it when we were courting. Enoch knew my thoughts and questions. How I questioned the restrictions on the roles women were allowed in the church. I felt safe talking to him... When I hadn't really talked to anyone about it, other than my *Mamm* and *Daed*."

Gulping back a sob, she went on, "He's actually told me not long ago that he was so against it, so afraid of my going on *rumspringa* because he thought I might not come back. That's why he didn't write me when I was in Baltimore with Uncle Brandon!"

She finished on another sob and had to take a minute to gather herself—wiping away her tears as they fell.

While she did this, her friend looked down, saying "You know, Kate, maybe that's why he didn't give you the letter. It was wrong of Enoch, but he...might still have been afraid."

"Maybe, but how can I trust him now?" She gulped in another breath. "I was raised in this world and I've cherished this life in many ways. And just now, I've found a real purpose, helping new mothers find their way. I had even hoped to have a child of my own soon enough. I mean I love Sarah, but I want to bear a *Boppli*. And I thought I would—Enoch's *Boppli*!"

"I know," Hannah patted her again as she sobbed quietly into a handkerchief.

Kate lifted her face. "I—I love Enoch, Hannah. I've always been drawn to him, but in these last few weeks, my heart has gone to live in his pocket! I love him—that's what hurts so much. I love him. Perhaps I always will, but I don't think I can trust him. I can't stay here, not knowing what else he'll lie to me about."

Looking at her steadily, Hannah said in a low voice, "You must do whatever you believe—and *Gott* tells you—is best."

"I do not believe," Kate said with resolution, "that God wants me and Sarah to stay in a home where I'm surrounded by lies. Perhaps this was all part of Enoch's revenge. He admitted he was angry that I went to Baltimore and angry that I married Jakob. All that and now his lie, I cannot believe he truly loves me. I think I must leave."

Hannah placed her hand on Kate's as it rested on the table. "If that is what you feel you should do. I will miss you, but you must do what you believe is God's will. Even if others' fail to understand it."

Meeting her friend's gaze, Kate said, "The bishop and elders here would not agree. They will tell you to shun me."

Sitting back in her chair with a sad smile, Hannah said, "The bishop cannot make this decision for you, Kate. This is your life."

"But, *Mamm,* why are we leaving? Is Papa Enoch not coming with us?"

Sitting on Hannah's bed the next morning, Kate stroked the brush again through the length of Sarah's white-blonde hair. "I know it's hard to understand, *Boppli,* but we must go to Baltimore with my uncle—and no, Enoch isn't coming with us."

The child was silent, standing submissively in front of Kate while she put down the brush and began twisting the long hair into a flat bun at the back of her small head.

Kate didn't even realize she was again crying until her vision blurred as she slipped in the pins to hold Sarah's hair in place. She wiped the back of a hand across her eyes, quickly drawing in the sob that threatened to escape.

She didn't want to leave, but she couldn't stay. Even if going meant leaving Hannah and her family. And Becca and little Isaiah.

"*Mamm?*" Sarah turned her head back to look over her shoulder. "Are you crying?"

If there was ever a moment God would forgive her for lying, Kate believed this was it. She forced a bright smile. "No, *liebling.* Turn back so I can finish putting on your *kapp.*"

"Are we," the child spoke slowly, "coming back soon?"

"I cannot say." Kate couldn't see a path to ever return to Enoch, but then she could see nothing beyond this day. She only had faith that God saw the way better than did she.

"So, this is..." Sarah hesitated, "like my Papa and like Grandpa James and Grandma Lizzie. We will not see Enoch again?"

Dropping the starched white *kapp* she'd started fitting on the child's head, Kate drew her into a hug, her chin on the little blonde head. "I'm so sorry, *liebling.* You've had to say too many goodbyes."

Not only was she taking Sarah from the new *daed* Kate had given her, they were leaving the world Sarah had grown up in. Everything she knew.

"Yes, Mam, but Enoch is not dead like Papa and Grandpapa," Sarah protested. "I saw him last night as we drove away. He stood on the front porch, watching us leave. I saw him."

"No," Kate responded in a voice that only wobbled a little, "he's not dead."

"Well, then, why can't he come to this place with your uncle?"

Picking up the small *kapp* from the bed, Kate said in a hard voice, "Enoch doesn't want to come to Baltimore."

"What is this place? And why hasn't your uncle visited us? He looks different. His clothes are not like ours and he was riding in a car, like some of the people in town do."

Sliding a pale clip into Sarah's hair to hold her *kapp* in place, Kate decided direct answers were the best way to respond to the girl. "Uncle Brandon isn't Amish like we are. He's like those people in town. He's *Englisch*."

"*Englisch?* And that's why Papa Enoch won't visit him?"

"Yes. Partly." She brushed a piece of fuzz off the girl's skirt. There was no way she'd tell Sarah that Enoch didn't really love them. That he'd married her and brought them into his home only to lie to Kate.

She couldn't tell little Sarah that Enoch thought no more of women than did most of the men of the Amish order. Thought of them as possessions, like cattle. She'd thought he was different. A bitter, bitter surprise had sat in her stomach since she'd turned from greeting her uncle and seen the truth on Enoch's face.

He'd treated her just as if she had no right or capacity to make her own choices.

"Then why are we going to Baltimore? If Papa Enoch won't come?"

"Hush, child," Kate said, angry tears again prickling behind her eyes. "You must trust me. Now go on out to play with the others."

"Yes, *Mamm*." The girl went to open the bedroom door, stopping to ask, "Do you think your uncle has a buggy? One I might get to drive?"

"I don't think so, Sarah. You go play now."

Her daughter had no conception that she was leaving more in this life than the buggy. Kate watched her go, acknowledging her own gripping uncertainty that this was the best choice. She took not only Sarah, but herself away from everything and everyone they knew. The life that had sheltered them and helped them find God.

Brought her a community and a role—albeit one that was too often restrictive—and a simple connection with the God she relied on.

Only now Enoch had thrown everything up in the air. Just when she'd begun to see a place for herself in her world, a purpose and a way she could do godly work. She knew she'd helped Becca and by providing support to a new—overwhelmed—mother, she'd found what had felt like her job in life.

And her man.

Only Enoch had proven by his deceit…and his complete lack of faith in her that he couldn't love her. Not really.

"I think Kate is leaving." Isaac leaned over to say.

Walking around the house the next morning with a sick feeling in his midsection, Enoch said, "Thanks, brother."

He walked heavily toward the door, seeing Kate putting a satchel into the Hostetler buggy. Enoch hated her for leaving him,…but he loved her more than his next breath.

Barely aware that his brother had disappeared into the barn, Enoch walked to the buggy outside his house as John Hochstetler got in to the driver's seat. At the buggy's open door, Kate stood, stuffing items inside.

"You're leaving now? You have everything you need?" Even though everything inside of him wanted to grab her and haul Kate back into the house—where he could keep her always at his side— Enoch knew he couldn't. He loved her and that meant accepting her choices.

She didn't look at him, continuing to rearrange the things in the buggy. "Yes. For now."

Aching at the gulf he'd created between them, Enoch cleared his throat before saying, "Don't worry about getting the rest— anything you couldn't get now. You can get it whenever you want."

Kate glanced over to meet his gaze then, her blue eyes dark with trouble.

Feeling he might never see her again, he stared at her as if he could burn her image on his brain. She was so lovely...and he was such a jackass.

"Thank you." She shut the buggy door, exchanging a long look with him.

Enoch had never felt more reproached—for his deceit, for never telling her how much he loved her. For his own faithlessness...in both God and her.

"Okay." With that word, she walked around and got in the buggy.

Watching it drive away with his heart, Enoch had never felt less okay in his life. He stood staring at the diminishing black buggy until it disappeared around the bend in the road...and she was gone.

Turning back to the barn, he went inside, swallowing hard as he leaned back on the rough door.

"Is it done?" Samuel sat on a stool beside the stalls.

"She's left, *Daed*." Enoch straightened from the door to pace across the barn in front of the stalls. "You were here yesterday when her uncle came. You saw the whole ugly scene."

"Yes." His father positioned himself on a bale. "I was not far from the door when the man came in."

Enoch swung around to face Samuel. "Kate spent the night at Hannah and John Hostetler's. She wouldn't even stay to hear what I had to say."

"I imagine not, son." His father looked at him with a sad expression.

"Yes." Bitterness and regret clashed in Enoch's stomach. "Kate went inside with John Hochstetler and got hers and Sarah's things. She said when she first got here with John that she and Sarah are going with her uncle."

"You've spoken with her?"

"Yes." A gust of air escaped Enoch. "Some. I tried. She won't listen to me, though."

"What did she say?" Gesturing toward the barn door, Samuel said, "Isaac will be out feeding your animals for a while yet. You can talk freely."

Settling onto a bale of hay near his father, Enoch stared sightlessly at the door his father had gestured toward. "I need to thank Isaac. I'm glad you both came this morning. I haven't been able to think beyond doing the basic chores."

It seemed strange to think of everyday things. Of course, farmers had to feed their lifestock, but nothing seemed right.

"You love Kate." His father concluded shrewdly, his gaze on his son. "It doesn't always happen this when a man marries a woman. There is often a Godly appreciation of her worth, but not always this."

Shaking his head, Enoch sighed heavily before saying, "Yes, father. I do. I—I didn't know how much when I accepted her proposal after her parents died. Not really. Even though I courted her years ago."

"When you and Kate were courting in your younger years and things went badly between you—before she went on *rumspringa* and ended up marrying Jakob—I never said anything."

"I know and I appreciate that, *Daed*."

"You were sweethearts, although no one else knew that when you were courting, and you were so happy in the beginning. So fitting together, it seemed—and then when she ended up marrying Jakob Beiler. Well, you seemed...to go away. Your happiness, I mean."

Enoch just looked at the old man, nothing inside of him besides regret. If only he'd handled her *rumspringa* differently. If he'd just written her in response to her letter to him.

"I've been a fool, *Daed*. I've handled this badly from the start. And particularly this last part. Just when we were getting close. We were married and happy together." Enoch looked down to where his fingers had worried several pieces of straw from the bale. "I should have told her before about the letter. I should have trusted God and given it to her. It's too late now."

"You do love her, my son. I can see that." His back leaning against the barn wall, he met his son's eyes.

"Yes, of course, I do," admitted Enoch heavily. "Not that it makes any difference at this moment."

A sliver of bitterness sliced through him. "And she's left. Again. As I always thought she might."

Despite his wanting her not to leave for *rumspringa*, she'd gone. And again she'd driven away from him. He knew his own actions had been wrong, but the irony of her leaving wasn't lost on him.

"Despite my love for her, she's leaving." Enoch looked up to his father's level gaze. "Not that I've ever told her of it. Not really. Not in so many words. Maybe that's for the best. I don't know."

"Why haven't you told her? To have this kind of thing spoken is important to women."

Smiling at the irony of his father telling him this when his father, to Enoch's knowledge, had never courted anyone other than his mother, he said, "I guess…I guess I wanted to protect myself."

He looked up again. "I've never felt anything like this before. That's what scared me when I got the letter. I didn't want to care. There has never been another woman in all these years—even after Kate married Jakob—who I could see as my wife. But still, I…feel this way toward her."

Scrunching down on the bale of hay, he said with caustic humor, "I know that makes me sound like a chicken heart."

Samuel laughed. "Son, it makes you sound like a man. It takes a brave heart to admit to that kind of weakness."

CHAPTER ELEVEN

Sweat running down to plaster his shirt to his back, Enoch again swung the ax. When chunks of wood fell to the ground around the tree stump he used for splitting wood, he bent to pick them up before tossing the pieces toward the growing pile.

"Are you just going to keep going at the wood pile?" Isaac sat on a rock over to the side. He'd walked over, unexpected and unannounced this morning, to sit watching Enoch split wood.

That his brother knew about Kate's departure wasn't even a question. Isaac would have heard about it from someone, even if he'd left the meeting early. Enoch knew his marital situation was the talk of the area. His father might be discreet, but the rest of the community wouldn't be able to resist.

Sliding his hand forward on the ax handle again, Enoch lifted it high over his head and let it fall again with a resounding *thwak*, slicing deep into the chunk on the stump in front of him. Salty droplets rolled down the center of his back and he ran a hand over his forehead, wiping at the dampness.

Even the winter chill couldn't cool him. After having started chopping wood two hours before, he could feel the heat rolling off him. He was hot, except for the chill around his heart and he'd done that to himself. His muscles ached after splitting firewood for so long, but even that was better than thinking.

She was gone. Again Kate had left him for the *Englisch* world. He should have seen this coming—before marrying her. Before losing even more of his heart. In trying to keep her—hold her with him—he'd committed the sin of deceit. At least, he knew that's what it was in God's eyes.

If only it didn't feel he had a hole in his heart, now that she was gone.

Again, he raised the ax and brought it down, thudding against the dry, cold timber.

"This wood has good grain." He ran his hand over a piece. When his brother didn't respond, Isaac leaned back to rest his outstretched arm on another part of the rock that supported him, his sheepskin jacket fastened snug around him. "What did that wood ever do to you?"

Enoch didn't respond to this facetious question. He'd always liked Isaac before, even when his younger brother was an annoying childhood tagalong... Until now. Now he didn't need to be bothered by anyone.

It was all he could do to breathe. He just focused on breathing...and beating this wood to death, piece by piece.

"Are you going after her?"

Enoch rested the ax head on the stump. "What?"

"Are you going after Kate?" Isaac repeated himself slowly as if he were speaking to someone with mental limitations. "Or maybe I should ask when you're going after her."

"Why would I do that?" snapped Enoch, turning back to lift the ax again. "She's where she wants to be."

His brother waited until he'd brought the sharp blade down heavily, again biting sharply into the block of wood in front of him. It sank deep, the block splitting in half.

As he bent to pick up the pieces of wood, tossing them on to the growing pile, Isaac said simply, "Because you love her, foolish brother. And Kate belongs here."

"She doesn't believe she belongs here." His reply shot out. "And she gets to decide that."

Isaac chuckled. "No. Not really. God decides where we belong...and everything indicates He wants her here. With you."

The words pierced Enoch's chest and he ached with it...with missing Kate. And little Sarah's bright face. Her laughter when he tickled behind her ear. He thought even old Betsy seemed more depressed without Sarah's attention.

"I guess if God wants Kate here, He'll bring her here."

Isaac got up from the rock, slapping several brown, wrinkled leaves off his pants. "Maybe God wants you to be His servant. To convince her that she and Sarah belong here. With you. Maybe she needs to know you're sorry for keeping that letter from her."

"Have I said I'm sorry?" His words came out with an angry snap.

Bringing the sharp blade of his axe down on another chunk of wood, Enoch let the tool come to rest on the sod beside his foot. He looked at his brother—who hadn't responded to the question—his chest rising to suck in the cool air.

"No." Isaac looked at him, unimpressed by his anger. "No, you haven't, brother. But nothing else would have you out here beating at the woodpile this way.

Saying nothing, Enoch watched the younger man put his hat on his head, as if he were leaving. He was sorry—very sorry. If he could do it all over, he'd give her the letter and rely on her—and God—to make all good.

"What makes you think I could convince her of that? I tried and failed to keep her here with me when we were youngies. It appears I've failed again at the same task."

Shifting his hat to settle it more securely, Isaac smiled at him. "Maybe this time you'll be doing God's work and He'll be with you."

Kate climbed the chilly bus steps, glad to get her and Sarah out of the sharp wind. She paused at the meter box, "Driver, is this the right coin?"

Just getting to the food store was strange and complicated here.

Taking his curt nod for what it was worth, she turned and started down the bus aisle, a shrinking Sarah clinging to her hand.

She knew now they were here in the *Englischer* world, she had to become accustomed to the stares as her dark, simple dress was longer than most around her and strange to others. She and Sarah still wore their starched linen prayer *kapps*.

"Excuse me. Excuse me," she murmured as she swayed along the drafty bus, trying to make their way to an empty seat as it started off again. The bus smelled of exhaust and sweaty people. Never had she longed more for the wide open fields of home. Never had she been angrier with Enoch. It burned inside of her, making her nights sleepless and hovering over her like a dark cloud.

Because of him, they couldn't go back. She had conflicts over the role she was allowed in the church, but at least before she'd thought he loved her. Here she was again, at Uncle Brandon's...pining for Enoch. She clearly wasn't making a lot of progress.

Just the thought made her angrier at him.

"*Danke*—thank you." She moved along the aisle, the German word slipping out of her mouth before she realized it.

A dark-skinned woman a little older than her smiled at Kate, gesturing for another woman to move from a seat across the aisle, leaving a spot for Kate and the child. Balancing as best she could while the woman's friend moved to sit next to the woman, Kate smiled her gratitude as she shifted Sarah into the now-empty seat, occupying the aisle side herself.

"Hi," the woman said, her smile still friendly, "I'm Tiffany Sampersand. I haven't seen you around here before. You're new to this neighborhood, aren't you?"

"Yes," Kate returned the smile across the aisle, glad to find a friendly local. "My little girl and I have only been here a few days."

Tiffany looked curious. "You're Amish, aren't you?"

Kate had thought about adopting an *Englischer's* garb so she and Sarah didn't stand out so much, but it just hadn't felt right.

"Yes, I'm Kate and this is Sarah, my daughter. We're here staying with my uncle." For a week? Forever? She just didn't know and she couldn't seem to think right now. Thank God, Uncle Brandon hadn't asked.

"I-I know we look strange to most." She put a self-conscious hand up to press against her chest.

Tiffany sent her a dry smile. "What? Because you don't wear dresses up to your hoohah? We don't mind that at all, do we, Shakirah?"

"Not at all." The woman on the other side of her nodded, smiling shyly as she shook her head.

"Why there's women—and those who may or may not be women—walking up and down these streets like they be advertising what they got." Tiffany lifted her shoulders peaceably.

Chuckling in response to the woman's expression, Kate realized suddenly that she hadn't laughed since her uncle showed up at the house. Not since she'd left Enoch...who'd lied to her and treated her like a child. Enoch, who she wanted to strangle.

Sternly steering her thoughts away from her husband, she forced herself to widen her smile, even though her heart was not happy. "Tiffany, Sarah and I have a grocery shopping list. Where do you recommend we go?"

"Here." Tiffany reached out for the slip of paper. "Let's see. We don't want you spending too much money or going to some of those questionable stores. You be proper ladies."

She gestured at the list in her hand, lifting it for her friend to see. "Yes, see here, Sapphira? I think B & B Groceries ought to have everything. You two just get here? This list looks like a move-in list. Seems to cover everything, 'cept cleaning stuff. Do you need cleaning supplies?"

Kate shook her head. "No, Uncle Brandon's place is clean. It just doesn't have food."

"Oh, that's right. You said you're staying with your uncle." Tiffany adjusted her big purse more comfortably on her lap. "Well, that's good. It's always nice to see relatives getting along."

Nodding again, Shakirah piped up to say, "My uncle lives with two of his brothers."

Sitting next to her, Tiffany gave her a dry look. "Yeah, but not because they get along."

Both women started cackling and their laughter was so infectious, Kate found herself smiling, too.

The bus exhaust smell wasn't as strong here and even though Sarah's hand still clung to hers, it wasn't as chilly back in the middle of the bus as when they'd first gotten on. She sat on the cracked vinyl seat with the child still huddled next to her, and found herself wondering what Enoch was doing back home.

She was so angry, she wanted to yell at him...

Angry, too, that being so angry didn't mean she didn't want to kiss him.

"There's a seat over here, Enoch." Hannah gestured to the side. "I'm glad you came."

Enoch nodded, shifting toward the empty seats. He'd avoided the church gathering after Kate and Sarah left, but the ache inside him wouldn't go away. Time did nothing for it and he was seeking comfort in God. It was all he knew to do.

"Here, son. Come sit with your brother and I." Samuel gestured toward him.

Sliding into the chair next to his father, Enoch cleared his throat and commented to Isaac, who sat in a chair on the other side of their *Daed*, "What are you doing here? Don't you usually sit with your girl?"

Kate and Sarah had been gone a week and a half. He didn't think he'd slept through one night, the bed next to him empty... His life empty.

"Rebecca Schrock and I have decided not to keep courting." Isaac kept his voice low as it wasn't their way to announce courtships. The two had never announced or acknowledged to the community that they were courting. "Besides, I sat with all the younger church members, not just her."

153

Enoch lifted his brows, noting that the news didn't seem a surprise to their father. "But now you have the urge to sit here with *Daed*?"

"Yes," Isaac hissed under his breath. "I do. Anything wrong with that?"

"No." He had no need to give his brother grief. Enoch was so caught up with the hole in his chest that he didn't particularly want to add Isaac's trials to it.

"I'm glad you have come to be with us," Samuel said, briefly pressing his son's hand. "This is a good place to be."

As the sermon commenced, Enoch let the bishop's words roll over him. There was peace in the continuity of it all. The sameness of these gatherings. He'd sat listening to sermons since he was a boy. Even though his insides now felt like churned butter, he felt a little comforted to sit next to his father and one of his brothers in the same kind of service he'd known since he was a child.

He'd sat in church gatherings like this after Kate went on her *rumspringa*, so afraid—so filled with anger at his fear—that he'd only made things worse. He knew God was with him then, but Enoch was sure he hadn't been open to hear God's voice during that terrible time. As bitter as that had been, this was worse. Now he had only himself to blame. Not Jakob. He couldn't even blame Kate.

He was the one who'd hidden the letter. Discarded it, so she wouldn't know her uncle had responded to her plea.

After the sermon was over, Kate's friend, Hannah came over to where Enoch stood aimlessly waiting for a seat to open at a table. She pulled him into a strong one-armed hug.

"How are you, Enoch?"

His smile felt tired. "How do you think, Hannah?"

The woman gave him another motherly hug, not answering.

"Have you heard from her?" Feeling compelled, he said, "She hasn't answered a single one of my letters."

"Oh," the woman lifted her eyebrows in question, "this time you wrote?"

He felt himself flush, conscious of and ashamed of his actions, "Hannah, you know I've always loved her. I wish I had written back then."

She shifted back a little to look at him. "How was I to know that, Enoch? You are not a man to show on his face what he feels inside. It can be hard to tell. Even though we are counseled to pour out our griefs to God, nowhere does it say to keep your heart from others."

"You know, I do—" he paused to clear his throat. "I do love her. I always have. These things are private—we don't make a show before the world of what we feel. We live simple, plain lives."

"You don't need to parade yourself in front of others, but telling your wife how you feel is certainly appropriate."

"I know." He turned to face Hannah more squarely, "I have been…showing her that I love her. I believe Kate knows."

"But you kept the letter from her."

Hannah's words were simple.

"Yes," Enoch said, "I did."

"*Daed*," Enoch said, as he drove Samuel home after the church service, "what shall I do? I-I cannot even breath without her. I do not know how to go on."

Isaac had brought the older man to the church service, but Enoch was glad to drive his *Daed* home. He felt churned up, having been at the service without Kate. Everywhere he was without Kate, he couldn't drag his mind off her absence.

This disarray was foreign to him. When she'd left before—and married Jakob when she got back—Enoch had shifted his loss to anger. Now, he couldn't even do that. Yes, he was angry that she was gone, but if she came back, he'd cup her face in his hands and kiss her madly. He was that gone.

It was a good thing old Betsy knew her way home because the reins were slack in Enoch's hands.

"My son," his father sent him a kind smile. "I understand. I didn't know how to live after your mother died."

"Yes, of course." He also missed his *Mamm*. Ruth Miller had been the cornerstone of their family, the one to whom they'd all turned. They all missed her loving warmth. "I'm a sad replacement for her kind wisdom," Samuel said, "but I think I know what your *Mamm* would say to you now."

Turning to look at his father, so familiar with his flowing white beard, his dark felt hat resting on crisp, gray locks. "What would she tell me?"

"It is so simple, my son." Samuel turned to look at him steadily. "Your *Mamm* would counsel you to pray to God. Only through His guidance and His forgiveness can you find the right path."

Looking back at the familiar road, Enoch said, "I do pray. It is custom and I have always found comfort in that."

"You pray," his father said, "but have you asked for forgiveness? Have you brought an open heart before the Lord and asked for His direction?"

Enoch didn't know how to answer. He'd prayed everyday—both before Kate left and after—but he still felt ashamed of his actions. And he still didn't know how to heal the breach with her, if that was even possible.

"My son, God will help you know what to do."

Two hours later, Enoch stood in the cold, drafty barn, rubbing old Betsy down. Beneath his strokes, her warm horseflesh quivered and twitched and a thin beam of sunlight filtered it's way through the fine straw dust motes. With even, steady passes, he worked her over as he had so many times before, the steamy horse smell of her a faint sort of comfort.

It was all very good for his *Daed* to talk of prayer, but Enoch felt he'd so transgressed that even God looked down on him with less than kindness. Kate certainly did. Only how did he survive this? How did he keep going on caring for the farm and the chickens. The hollow spot in his chest kept getting bigger, not smaller. He didn't know how else to fill it.

Leaning his head forward on Betsy's warm back, the scent of horse filling his nose, Enoch prayed from his heart, his simple words whispering through the quiet barn.

"God, I am a foolish man. You are Almighty and wonderful to love us. But I did not trust You to do what was best. I schemed to keep Kate with me. I am broken, God. You know this. I cannot go on without her. Please, God, tell me what to do."

CHAPTER TWELVE

Kate sat on her uncle's couch a week later, a book open in her hands. Uncle Brandon—home from his job for the day—sat at the other end of the small, red couch, his eyes on the program on the television in front of them.

She'd read the same page of the book twice already, but she slogged on, hoping she'd eventually get lost in the favorite tale. The voices on the television murmured something, but she wasn't paying attention. At a small table in the condo's adjoining eating area, Sarah quietly colored on paper.

Her uncle murmured, his voice pitched low, "Has Enoch written you? If you don't mind my asking? I've noticed you bring in the mail."

Startled, she glanced over to meet his gaze. "No, he hasn't."

Reaching over a warm hand to cover hers, the older man said, "You and Sarah are welcome here, Kate. As long as you want. You know that. Whenever you're ready, if you'd like I have a friend who can offer you a job. It's not much, but I don't think making meals for little Sarah and I truly occupies your mind."

Kate blinked back a tear and huffed out a sigh. "Not really. I love cooking, but…"

Her uncle had almost been like a father to her these past few weeks, but the days had been long and strangely purposeless. Despite knowing she shouldn't…she missed Enoch terribly.

Straightening to pull his hand back to his lap, Uncle Brandon sent her an encouraging smile. "I know this is a difficult time for you. Let me know if I can help. Tell me what you want to do."

"*Danke.*" She wasn't sure what else to say. In truth, her mind and heart were in such a jumble that she had no direction at this point. Leaving home—and Enoch —had been a gut reaction for her.

He'd lied to her! Deceived her.

It made no sense in the face of things, but she missed both her former life…and him. She felt paralyzed and didn't know what to do.

Going back home with her tail between her legs seemed unacceptable. For all she knew, Enoch had gone to the elders to complain of her departure and she even now faced their displeasure. No one in their area had been shunned in many, many years, but everyone knew exactly what it meant.

To turn her back on the faith? On worshipping God in a simple, plain life?

The thought made her shudder. Not only because she'd be shut off from her friends, from Hannah and Rebecca, but because the life she'd loved would be blocked from her forever.

As would Enoch.

And this would be even worse than the period during which she'd been married to Jakob. At least then, she'd seen Enoch at church gatherings. She'd known he was safe and alive. If she wasn't there, she could know nothing of him.

She both craved and resented Amish life. The simplicity of warm friendship, the basics of living a daily life of God. But all her days, she'd seen her mother—her educated intelligent mother—hide her light under a bushel. It had seemed wrong and even though Elizabeth Lehman had laughed when she dismissed Kate's observations, Kate had never made peace with the Amish tolerance of women attending only to houses and having babies.

Even though he'd done such a terrible thing, she craved Enoch. The warmth of his strong embrace. The wonderful smell of his skin. The sound of his breathing as he slept beside her.

Of course, she'd felt a purpose in helping Rebecca. That part of being an Amish woman had felt good. It had also given an outlet for her own longing. One she didn't talk about. She loved Sarah fiercely, but she just as fiercely wanted to add to her family—a child of hers and Enoch's. A babe from her body.

Being conceived of a child would make this current decision a little clearer. She'd have felt it to be God's will that she forgive him and return to raise their child together.

Not that he'd asked for forgiveness. The jerk.

In the weeks that had passed since she'd come to stay here, Kate had secretly hoped and believed that she was in fact pregnant at last. Pregnant with Enoch's child, she'd return to the life she always loved, even though conflicted about some parts.

She couldn't steal his child away.

He'd be a wonderful father...particularly if the child was a boy. If she were honest with herself, Enoch had been a wonderful father to Sarah of late. Once the awkwardness between them passed—teaching her to drive the buggy and letting her work with wood in the barn alongside him.

But this morning she'd risen to find she'd started her monthly flow. She wasn't pregnant; she was still stuck in this place— unsure how to proceed and her longing to bear a child ungratified.

How could she forgive Enoch when he'd betrayed her so? He to whom she'd confided her concerns and questions. She couldn't just ignore that he'd treated her as if her opinions didn't matter. How was this any different from his insistence she not go on a *rumspringa*?

On top of that, since their marriage, he'd started acting like the loving man she knew from before, but he'd never actually said he loved her. Not in so many words.

It probably didn't make sense, but that mattered.

Three weeks after Kate left, Enoch stepped off the Greyhound bus, reaffirmed after riding in the vehicle for a long thirteen hours that he wasn't meant for the *Englischer* world.

After talking with his father–and later hearing Isaac's views whether he wanted to or not—it had come to Enoch forcibly in the night that he hadn't done his part in the marriage. It was almost as if God's voice spoke to him, the realization crashing into his consciousness.

Having come to that conviction, he'd had a hard time waiting till he could get a bus into Baltimore. He had to see Kate.

Enoch stood on the cold tarmac outside the bus terminal, the bus fumes all around him, and he knew he had to tell Kate how he felt. Before, he'd been so consumed with the injustice of his actions, with his commitment to stop telling her what to do, that he'd believed he had no right to say anything. He'd watched her drive away, his heart fading away.

Prayer and his father's and brother's counsel had shown him, though, that he hadn't yet done his full part. This wasn't about telling Kate what to do. This was about letting her choose. She had the right.

Even if she refused to forgive him and chose to continue in this life, he hadn't given his all to the marriage. In the dark of night as he paced the floor again, praying that God would send him a signal, he realized this as clearly as a board upside the head. He'd always been running scared with Kate.

From the beginning when he tried to block her from going on *rumspringa* to now. Fear of losing her had kept him from trusting God—trusting her—and driven all his actions. Hiding her letter had been wrong, but he was more wrong in not going to her before to beg her forgiveness. She still had the choice of whether or not to return to their life together, but she deserved to hear the whole story. She needed to hear him confess his love.

He walked across to the bus terminal building, his father's worn suitcase in his hand and looked for a cab.

"But Kate," Uncle Brandon said through the bedroom door an hour later, "he's here and he wants to speak with you."

Sitting on the bed with her hands clenched together, she stared blindly ahead, tears tracking down her cheeks, her body flushed with warmth.

"Won't you come out and talk with him?"

In the kitchen cleaning up when she heard her uncle open the door to Enoch's knock, she'd recognized the timbre of his voice immediately and fled to the bedroom. "I don't know," she quavered in a shaky voice. "I don't know what to do."

If Enoch had come here with the stern intent of dragging her and Sarah back—the thought both infuriated her and left her shamefully excited—she couldn't speak to him.

"What?" Her uncle's voice was muffled by the door.

"Give me a moment," she called out in a lifted voice. It wasn't fair or reasonable to tremble here when her uncle and her daughter were out there with Enoch. She was ashamed of her reaction. She should stand before him like the angels with flaming swords had stood at the gates of the Garden of Eden. Maybe Enoch hadn't committed the sins of Adam and Eve, but he'd still broken their relationship.

Standing, she went to the mirrored chest-of-drawers and gazed at her image to shakily straighten her *kapp* and tuck dark strands of her hair in more firmly beneath it. "I'm coming, Uncle."

She opened the bedroom door and went out, throwing a reassuring smile at her uncle who stood beside the door with an anxious look on his worn face. If only she felt as confident. Pinning the smile on more firmly, she swung around to face Enoch.

He seemed to shrink the small condo living area by his size, although he was kneeling to the child's level with his hat in his hand as Sarah chattered away to him, his dark head bent to listen to her. Slowly, he straightened, his normally calm face looking surprisingly nervous.

"Kate." He took a short step toward her, stopping before he'd moved completely away from Sarah. "You look...beautiful. As always."

She drew in a short breath, trying to calm her jittery stomach. "Thank you."

Uncle Brandon surged forward, gathering up Sarah's colors and urging her around. "Come on, sweetie. Let's go in the bedroom to finish your drawing."

Within a short moment, Kate stood alone facing the man who'd betrayed her.

"Kate," he started to say, his eyes on her face, "I messed up everything between us. Again."

"What do you mean?" Her throat felt tight and breathing was difficult. She knew, of course, but she wanted to hear him own it. He never should have hidden her letter.

"I-" He cleared his throat and started again, "I told you I was afraid of you going on *rumspringa,* that some *Englischers* would woo you."

"Yes."

"What I haven't said—what I should have told you was that I've always been—" Enoch hesitated again. "I've always been afraid of what you made me feel. Always. From the first when we started courting."

"I...I don't know what you mean."

He stepped closer, now within arms' reach. "Kate, you make me—not myself. And more myself. Hot inside and jealous. When we were first courting, I worried until I saw you and then when we were together, I dreaded that I had to leave to go home."

He paused, his fingers worrying his hat. "I've always feared you leaving me."

Unable to process his words or the dark fire burning in his eyes, Kate just stood there in the small living room, looking at him, a flood of disbelief and joy coursing through her.

Words seemed to explode from him then, rapping out with intensity. "A man isn't to feel this way about anyone—except maybe God. I burned inside to be with you. To touch your hand, your hair. Our kisses made me...almost unable to control myself. I had to pray for strength."

He turned and paced to the other side of the small condo living room to wheel back around to say, "I've always wanted...everything from you, Kate. From the first. You made me...feel things...and think of you much too often. You make me smile and laugh. You make me crazy with your sometimes irrational comments."

Rooted to the floor as his words flowed over her, she felt her heart thumping joyfully in her chest.

"What—what are you saying?" Her chest felt tight with hope. "That...these feelings made you...deceive me? Cut me off back when we were *youngies*?"

"Yes! Something like that. I mean, I was stupid. I didn't know how to handle everything you made me feel. I love you...and I've hated you." He said it with an urgent spurt. "I didn't write when you came here on *rumspringa* for the reason I told you and more."

Feeling tears of joy rush to her eyes, spilling over onto her cheeks, she threw up her hands to cover her face. He loved her! Still! Could she forgive him for his actions? His hiding her letter? Could she trust him?

Coming back to the middle of the room, his felt hat still clutched in his hand, Enoch stopped. "You unsettle me, Kate. When you came home and married Jakob, I was furious...and told myself I should be relieved. That I'd take a wife who didn't have this strange effect on me. That I'd be happy without you!"

The last was said with savagery and he stood in her uncle's living area, glaring at her.

"I used to worry that you'd marry." It was a breathless, shameful admission. She hadn't confessed that to anyone. "That I'd have to watch another woman be your wife."

The corner of his mouth lifted in a dark, wry smile. "Well, you didn't have to worry about that because no other girl interested me. Oh, I tried. It just didn't matter. None of them mattered."

She smiled then, catching at her shaky breath. "I prayed for forgiveness because I knew I shouldn't want you to be alone. But I didn't want you to be with anyone other than me."

Moving to her then, he took her chin in his cupped hand. "It drove me insane to see you with Jakob. I kept trying to marry someone—anyone—hoping to stop caring about you."

With him so close she could feel the warmth of his body, Kate felt herself tearing up and whispered, "I'm sorry. I'm sorry."

"Jezebel. Temptress." He murmured, turning his hand to let the back of it coast over her cheek. "I mourned when your parents died. I miss your *Daed* to this day, but I thought it might be easier for me if you moved to be with the Bieler family. Only you didn't. You came to me and proposed."

With the back of his hand still against her cheek, he narrowed his eyes and repeated slowly. "You...proposed to me."

"Yes."

Enoch dropped his hand, still standing close. She considered throwing her arms around his shoulders and burying her nose in his neck to inhale his scent, but she didn't want to chance him stopping talking. Katie said, "I'd been in a marriage that wasn't happy. I couldn't imagine taking a husband other than you."

"You proposed to me." He repeated, his dark eyes intense on her. "I told myself that this was my moment of revenge. That I could take you as my wife finally...and not love you. Be cool and distant. Not let you have this mad effect on me."

Dropping his head briefly to rub his hand over his face, Enoch straightened with his wry smile. "But I couldn't do it. I couldn't even remain distant from that imp, Sarah, and she's not your flesh."

Realizing her smile was growing broader, Kate said with as much demureness as she could muster, "Well, she is pretty loveable."

Taking her hand and maneuvering them over to sit down, he said, "I'm here to tell you all this—I love you—and to ask you to come home, Kate. With me. You and Sarah belong with me."

Enoch shifted her hand in his and started again. "I want to make sure I tell you I know I was wrong to destroy your letter. It was wrong of me on so many levels, Kate. I let my fear of losing you overrule my good judgment, my faith in you and in God."

165

"You actually thought that having married you, I would have left?" Kate made no attempt to pull her hand from his. "I love you. You must know that, Enoch."

He shrugged. "I knew you had questions about our life, the roles allowed to women. From what I could tell, you married me only because you had no other choice."

"I could have married Aaron Yoder," she murmured, tongue in cheek.

"Really? Could you have?" Enoch asked, cocking an eyebrow at her.

A giggle bubbled up in her. "Well, it would have been—no. I couldn't."

"After all," Enoch said, drawing her into his arms. "Aaron would expect you to be a good Amish wife through and through. I know you have a slightly unusual way of worshipping *Gott*, you renegade you.

With that he kissed her and she subsided happily into his arms. When she snuggled down against his broad shoulder, Kate said, "Take me home, Enoch. I'll never again leave you. No matter how frustrated I may get at times. You can trust me. Always."

Thanks so much for purchasing *Amish Renegade!* If you enjoyed this book, please consider leaving a review on your favorite retailer, and look for *Amish Princess*, the next in the series!

Read on for a special look at the next in the series, Amish Princess!

AMISH PRINCESS PREVIEW:

CHAPTER ONE

"Who is the pretty blonde girl sitting next to Martha Yoder? You know, Bishop Yoder's *Frau*." Isaac Miller asked his brother, Enoch, who sat in a chair beside him. Around them, the Amish Mannheim, Pennsylvania community chattered before the meeting started.

The Schwartz house grew warm as more families filed in for the worship service and the occasional woodsy puffs of smoke from the fireplace didn't help. Windows open to let in cool early spring breezes sent *Kapp* strings and beards fluttering as the hum of chatter filled the room, but probably also added to the gusts of acrid heat from the small fire. Rows of mismatched, serviceable chairs were filling as the noise of visiting neighbors rose around them.

A smirky smile eased onto Enoch's face. "You can see— under her black *Kapp*—that her hair is blonde?"

Rolling his eyes, Isaac admitted with a grin, "Of course. Do you know who she is or not? We can see by the dark *Kapp* that she's not married."

Leaning forward to look around her husband, Kate hissed, "She's the Yoder *princess*."

She managed to do this, holding baby Elizabeth over her shoulder and patting for a burb.

"What!? Princess?" Isaac yelped quietly. In their world, they believed themselves to be called by *Gott* to live simple lives of faith, dedication and humility. The Amish didn't believe in self-glory and even the idea of royalty was scorned. "The Yoder what?"

"You know," Kate said in a low voice, still patting the quietly-fussing *Boppli*, "Bishop Yoder's brother—the one living over at Elizabethtown—has five sons and only one daughter. Mercy. So they say she's been...coddled a bit. She's also the youngest of her family. Imagine a girl growing up with *five* protective big brothers?"

Flashing a glance at the pretty young woman sitting next to Martha Yoder, Isaac found himself asking his sister-in-law, "Why does she look so sad?"

Kate shrugged. "It is said that the *Mann* she was to marry—within weeks, mind you—ran away. Left the faith and disappeared into the *Englischer* world."

Blowing a soft puff of air through pursed lips, Isaac sat back. "That would trouble a girl."

"Do you two mind?" Enoch inserted his sardonic question from the chair between theirs, his eyebrows lifted.

Seeming unfazed, Kate shifted the *Boppli* to her other shoulder as she turned from her husband's admonishment to greet Samuel Miller, Isaac and Enoch's father who'd seated himself on her other side in the crowded room. "Welcome, *Daed* Miller!"

Even though Samuel was the father of six grown children and a widower, he was still strong and upright although going gray at his temples and his long beard held streaks of silver.

Isaac grinned a greeting at his *Daed* around Enoch and Kate.

"Good afternoon, *Dochder*." Samuel smiled back, leaning forward to tickle little Elizabeth's cheek. "It was too hot over with Lizzie and James, so I came to sit with you."

Ignoring the reference to his sister, Enoch again admonished them in a husky whisper to be quiet as Bishop Yoder stood in front of the congregation to offer the initial sermon. Bishop Yoder would yield later to Bishop King who would give the main sermon for the day.

Throughout the sermons, Isaac ignored his brother's occasional chin scratches—Enoch's beard was still growing in although he'd married Kate over a year ago. It was only natural, Isaac told himself, that his gaze occasionally strayed to where Mercy Yoder sat several rows in front of him. For a Yoder woman, she was remarkably attractive. Even with her black *Kapp* pinned in place, he could see the smooth wings of her blonde hair and the fine texture of her skin.

In a booming voice, the broad Bishop Yoder spoke of the belief that *Gott* decided their eternal end by weighing individuals' lifelong obedience to His rules against their disobedience. He thundered at moments and spoke his words quietly at others, his face stern above his gray beard.

Settled back in his chair to listen, Isaac idly glanced around the community of worshipers who rustled quietly as they also attended the *Mann* preaching. Even if Bishop Yoder did harbor ill thoughts against Isaac's family—since Kate had chosen to marry Enoch, rather than the Bishop's then-adolescent son, Aaron—he still had a strong message to share.

In the few moments between the first speaker and the second, Isaac asked his brother, "Where's Sarah?"

"Over with the other girls." Enoch nodded toward the area where a cluster of girls huddled on chairs, giggles erupting now that the speaker had stepped down.

"Silly *Maedel*," he said in a fond voice.

Ezekiel Schmidt stood to speak then and they fell silent again, giving him their attention.

When this sermon was finished nearly an hour later and several songs had been sung in the usual High German, Kate handed still-fussing *Boppli* to Enoch, probably preparing to go help the other women in the kitchen. Isaac knew feeding everyone was an enormous task often done in shifts, but Kate loved cooking, so this was no chore to her.

Just then *Frau* Hochstetler stopped by, her girth blocking the breeze from the window as she said in a dramatic under voice, "*Goedemorgen.* Have you seen the Yoder girl up there, sitting by Martha?"

"*Yah,*" Kate responded without enthusiasm.

"I have," Isaac said, looking back at beautiful Mercy Yoder with her blonde hair. He couldn't be sure from this angle, but he'd bet she had blue eyes, too.

"She's very pretty," the older woman said, her pale plump mouth primming, "but I hear the *Mann* she was to marry left his family in Elizabethtown and her—renouncing the church which he'd already joined—shortly before they were to say their vows. Just up and left. What can this say about her? No one knows why he left, but it can't help reflect on the Yoder girl. They call her the *princess* because she's had all these older brothers looking after her. And her parents, too. After five boys, the Yoders didn't think they'd have a *Dochder*."

Isaac felt himself turn to stone as he realized just who Mercy Yoder was... Who she had to be...and who she'd been betrothed to marry. Daniel Stoltzfus. She'd been preparing to marry Daniel. Why hadn't he realized this immediately when Kate had said who she was?

"I imagine not. I'm sorry, *Frau* Hochstetler, but I have to go help in the kitchen." His sister-in-law edged a little away from the woman.

Even though he was wrestling with his sense of guilt, Isaac watched with amusement as Kate tried to stem the garrulous woman's gossipy words.

"Of course! Of course. They say that the Yoder girl is to stay here with her uncle, Bishop Yoder, all summer. She gathers *wildflowers,* I've heard." This last was said with a repressive grimace, as though Rachel Hochstetler had something against wild blossoms. "She's supposed to make medicinal salves and potions from weeds and things. I don't know."

Her white *Kapp* pinned firmly enough not to move with the headshaking, the older woman rolled her eyes in emphasis.

Clearly trying to help his wife in an awkward moment, Enoch said, "That must be a blessing to some, if they are medicinal salves."

"*Yah,*" Rachel shrugged expressively. "She must do something to fill her hours, since she has no husband. I suppose *Gott* brings us every one to the right mate. At least, that what's said."

"Very true," Isaac responded with a grin.

"I must get to the kitchen," Kate tried again. "Excuse me, *Frau* Hochstetler."

"Of course. Of course." Rachel Hochstetler finally moved forward down the row.

"Well, *Bruder,*" Enoch turned to Isaac, jiggling the *Boppli,* "do you suppose this blonde Mercy Yoder is meant to marry Aaron?"

"You mean after Kate chose you instead? *Neh,* they are first cousins." Isaac slapped a goofy grin on his face, slipping automatically into his customary light-hearted banter.

Mercy Yoder had definitely been Daniel Stoltzfus' fiancée. In his unspoken shame, Isaac could only hope no one remembered that Daniel had spent several months in Mannheim at the Glick farm last year. Had Daniel told anyone what had led up to his leaving the Amish world? Surely not.

"It wouldn't be the first time cousins in our faith married." Enoch's mouth thinned. "Besides Aaron was too young for Kate. You know that."

Isaac elbowed his elder brother. "And she was still in love with you. Why else would she have asked you to marry her after her *Mamm* and *Daed* were killed in that buggy accident?"

Enoch smiled, looking very satisfied. "Bishop Yoder was still upset she didn't marry Aaron…even though he later counseled me to marry her."

"True, although it was his business as Bishop to help her work out what she'd do when widowed and alone after the deaths of her parents." Isaac laughed, throwing a glance at where the still-unmarried Aaron Yoder sat with several other young men. "Still, the Yoders have been frosty with the whole Miller family since then."

"That should put a crimp in your getting to know Mercy Yoder better," said Enoch with a dry smile.

Isaac leaned forward, his elbows on his knees. His gaze fell on the pretty girl sitting next to Martha. He felt a perverse desire—given his part in her situation—to get to know Mercy better. She was a beautiful woman, even when so sad. "It'll just make things more interesting."

"Not so much if this girl, Mercy, is meant to marry Aaron Yoder."

"Even if they weren't first cousins," Isaac cocked an eyebrow at his brother as he stood and turned toward the tables that had been set out for everyone to eat, "I'd still take my chances."

Later joining the stream of worshipers making their way to the tables that had been crowded into the house, he shifted and inched forward. As worship services were held in member homes, the rooms were packed with the faithful. A constant stream moved still through the narrow aisle between chairs as people jockeyed for places for the first sitting.

Isaac noted that as Zachariah Graber moved through the throng, he didn't look up or greet anyone, his face grim as usual. The old *Mann's Frau* had passed several years before and, his gray beard bristling angrily, he seemed to grow smaller and smaller with every day.

"Hello, *Frau*," Holding his straw hat loosely between his fingers as he passed by, Isaac bent to brush the other hand over the small boy's head. "Hello, little Abraham. Did you eat already?"

The tow-headed boy nodded vigorously as his mother said, "*Yah*. We're joining his *Daed* outside."

"*Gut*." Isaac nodded, as the woman passed by, her belly swollen with Abraham's brother or sister.

Walking into the room where tables had been set up, he looked to find himself a place to sit, now that the little ones had been fed. The room was growing warmer still with the press of people and the kitchen at the other side.

Continuing to thread his way through crowd, Isaac suddenly found himself looking into the blue eyes of Mercy Yoder. He'd been right. Her eyes were a beautiful blue, like the summer sky.

Standing face-to-face with the girl teasingly called an Amish *princess*, Isaac found a smile sliding onto his face.

The crowd of people shifted around them as one group moved from the tables and another took their places.

In the jostling transition several *youngies* brushed against black-*Kapped* Mercy Yoder and—thrown off balance momentarily—she leaned into Isaac.

He caught the rounded, feminine armful, a fresh, flowery scent filling his indrawn breath. How could Daniel Stoltzfus have left such a comely bride? No matter what had been said to him.

She glanced up at him, her summer-blue eyes startled. Snapping at him in a flustered way, she straightened herself. "Can you not watch where you're going?"

"I'm sorry," Isaac said, setting her back on her feet. "But the house is crowded and the *youngies* meant nothing."

"They should watch where they're going," Mercy said, starting to move away. "They could have knocked me to the floor!"

Isaac couldn't help grinning. "Then I'd have had to haul you from the floor. Not such a great distance...and thankfully you're not of an age to break a hip."

She brushed her skirt. "That's no excuse to rush past so carelessly."

Hurrying into speech as she turned away, he commented. "I saw you sitting next to *Frau* Yoder in the meeting earlier. That must mean you are the Yoders' niece. I heard you're here for the summer."

The blonde girl swung her blue gaze back to him, a faint, scornful smile playing around the corners of her mouth. Her brows lifted. "Because I sat beside her, I must be the niece?"

"Yes." His reply was swift as he grinned back at her. "We are a small town, here in Mannheim. I'm Isaac Miller and I've always liked the name Mercy."

With a tantalizing glimmer of a polite smile, she inclined her head, saying, "*Goedemiddag*, Isaac Miller."

With that, pretty Mercy Yoder turned and disappeared into the throng.

He watched her go, admiring her sassy response. This could be fun...even if he did feel a little guilty.

The next day, Mercy stroked her hand over the smooth, red, lance-shaped leaves of Lady's Thumb as a bright blue sky smiled overhead. A fresh late-spring breeze brushed tall field grass against her faded green dress. In her mind, she catalogued all the plant's benefits, remembering what her *Grossmammi* had taught her. *Heart ailments. Stomachaches and sore throats.* Gathering several leaves, she laid them flat in her basket. Today was less windy than the day before, bringing a more gentle movement to the grass swaying around her. She'd always loved wandering through the fields with her *Grossmammi,* the old woman filled with wisdom about treating health problems naturally. *Englisch* doctors were costly and often not found nearby. Using what was given by *Gott* to treat illnesses benefitted all.

To her surprise, Mercy suddenly noticed an elderly *Mann* had entered the field only yards from where she stood. Pausing to exchange a polite greeting, she stopped only to see him walk past, as if she weren't there. Hunched a little, he never turned his gray head or looked up from the path in front of him.

Mercy watched him as he walked to the edge of the field and left it through a break in some tree branches. He'd moved passed her as if he'd never seen her. Reflecting that the old *Mann* must have had a load on his mind since he hadn't noticed he wasn't alone, she continued on, occasionally bending to gather beneficial herbs.

As the youngest in her family, Mercy had spent a lot of time with the Yoder matriarch, deemed too young and fragile to work the farm. She could still remember her *Grossmammi* singing softly to her in Dutch as she went to sleep. As she'd gotten older, they'd crafted healing lotions and salves in their kitchen after Mercy's light work in the house and the home garden was done.

Pausing, Mercy sent up a prayer to *Gott*, thankful He'd taken her beloved *Grossmammi* into His arms after she'd left this world. She still missed the wise woman's words and comfort. If only *Grossmammi* Schwartz were here now to tell Mercy what to do, how to...move forward. How to survive the crushing mess around her.

She knew there were church members in Elizabethtown who'd thought too little was required of her, that hard work led individuals to live in *Gott's* way. They'd believed her pampered, and the remembrance of her whispered nickname—*princess*—bought a heated flush to her cheeks. Had Daniel seen her as a lightweight? Unable to do her part?

Had that been a part of why he'd left? The possibility troubled her.

After Daniel's defection—his choice to leave the life and leave her, too—she didn't know how to face everyone. She'd gone from feeling secure that her life was mapped out, safe and loved in the service of *Gott* and family...to having no aim. No purpose. No place.

Coming here to Mannheim to stay with *Onkle* and *Aenti* Yoder for the summer had been her parents' idea after dealing with the community curiosity and talk, a way to let the dust settle from Daniel's abandonment.

Mercy raised her chin a notch. There was no denying she felt stained by his actions, but she refused to let that define her. Even if she wondered how she'd not known he was that conflicted... How she'd missed any hint that the *Mann* she was courting and had planned to marry wasn't committed to this life.

Dusting her hands after crumbling a chunk of damp soil through her fingers, she stopped to lift her gaze to a puffy white formation of clouds above her. A brilliant blue above her, the sky seemed endless and Mercy suddenly wished she were a bird that could fly high above the land. The creatures of the sky didn't wonder if they were worthy, if they could meet the challenges of this world.

She didn't need anyone's pity, though. It wouldn't change anything and it caused hot embarrassment to crawl under her skin. What did Daniel's actions say about her and his dread of marriage to her? The question troubled her, but she certainly didn't need Levi, Caleb, Micah, Joseph or Elijah conspiring to find Daniel and *school* him. The Plain people valued a life lived *Gott's* way, a way of non-violence. Daniel might have left their world—and was now shunned for it—but that didn't mean her older brothers could twist his head off. They needed to recognize they couldn't protect her from desertion by the *Mann* she was to marry.

Picking a few more leaves to put in her basket, Mercy made mental note of the location, so she could come back if she needed. The cool breeze gently brushed the strings of her black *Kapp* against her neck. She'd attended the service with her *Onkle* and *Aenti* and prayed to *Gott*, but she felt…still tarnished.

It was as if, by leaving both her and the life they'd planned to share, Daniel had tilted her into this strange, uncertain place. As if she'd fallen short and failed at being a good wife before she even was one. Settling onto a stone in the glen, surrounded by stems of long prairie grass, she brought her knees up to her chin, the long skirt of her dress falling to her ankles.

Please, Gott. Help me find my way. Gott never abandoned his faithful.

It hadn't been her idea to spend the summer with *Aenti* and *Onkle* here in Mannheim, but her *Daed* had thought the time with his brother would spare her from hearing the whispers she knew were flying around their community. Even though she missed her family a lot, it was a relief not to feel the glances sent her way, both kind and curious.

And possibly—she thought of Isaac Miller's cheeky grin and broad shoulders as she'd walked away from him at the meeting—the summer might have some brighter spots.

A week later, Isaac brushed sawdust off the wood beneath his plane, before setting it again in motion. He loved the smell that rose from the wood he shaped.

"And what are you making this time," his *Daed* sat on a stool nearby, the woodshop windows thrown open to let in the late spring air.

"A bed. Hannah and John Hochstetler's little girl, Lydia, is ready for a bed of her own."

"Have they built onto the house? I didn't know they were expanding it or I'd have offered a hand. They already have four *Bopplis* in the one room." Samuel's brown hair was now heavily flecked with gray, but he could easily keep pace with his four sons when it came time to plow the fields or swing a hammer.

A light spring breeze wafted through the workshop.

"I think John's brothers pitched in. They said the frame didn't take more than a day." Isaac pushed the plane over the wood surface again, feeling the stretch of his muscles as he reached the length of the plank. This was all so familiar and soothing to him.

"Enoch and Kate said you were eying the pretty Yoder girl who is visiting Brother Hiram this summer. Do you think to win over even a Yoder female with your flirting?" His father's voice was indulgent.

Isaac pushed another curl of wood off the plank, letting a smile quirk the corner of his mouth. "Did they say that? Then maybe they were pulling your leg. You sat right there on the other side of Kate. If I was flirting, you'd have heard."

"She's a nice-looking girl," his father commented, a glimmer of Isaac's own teasing in his voice. "She might ignore her *Onkle's* warnings about us Millers, if you're sweet enough. Enough girls have, you *Schaviut.*"

"I'm grown out of my rascal phase. And, *yah,* she is comely. No doubt about it." Isaac squelched a smile. After all the teasing he'd done, he had no right to squawk when it came back his way. "Say, didn't you tell me you were going over to see James and Gideon?"

The rich scent of freshly-planed wood mixed nicely with the scent of blooming fruit trees just outside his shop and Isaac paused a moment to enjoy taking a breath. "I miss James and Gideon. I wish they were closer. You should go visit to make sure they're courting nice *Maedels*."

His other two brothers had both bought farms in a town a hundred miles away, since they'd found them at a good price, and visits between the relatives had to be planned.

Samuel shifted on the stool, ignoring Isaac's comments about his brothers with a smile both gentle and gleeful. "You might see this Mercy Yoder at the Sing that Kate and Enoch will host. She might teach you that you can't win all girls. You're too cocky by half, in this area. You need to find one woman. Settle down, get married to a good wife and work more on your farm, like your *Bruders*. All this furniture building is one thing, but the land will never let you down. It is *Gott's* way."

"Yes, *Daed*," Isaac finally grinned at his father, lifting the now smooth plank to lean it against the wall amongst others. "I know."

"You're not getting any younger, *der Suh*." Samuel Miller commented. "You've already joined the church. It's time you married and started a family. Maybe that Mercy Yoder is the right woman for you. You should at least pick one."

"Yes, *Daed*. And it would go over big with her *Onkle* if I picked that one, I'm sure. You know how the Yoders feel about Kate choosing to marry Enoch rather than their *youngie,* Aaron Yoder."

"Yes, but that kind of thing has never stopped you before. If a girl is pretty." his father told him.

"Well, if you do want to go see James and Gideon—to check up on how they're doing," Isaac said with a cheeky grin as he returned to his earlier question, "Enoch and I can watch over your place."

"I'm seeing them in the fall." His father got off the stool, brushing a stray curl of wood off his leg. "You and Enoch have your own land to watch in the planting and harvesting time. In the fall, the fields will be fallow. You'll have time to watch my farm and mess about with your wood. You can do both then. No reason to neglect your own farm."

Samuel stopped before exiting the workshop, throwing another smile toward Isaac. "I hope you have a good time at the Sing after this next service. You know, we Millers have never particularly cared about whether others like us or not."

As his father's footsteps receded, Isaac chuckled, continuing to shape the bed. The hush of the plane over wood had always been a peaceful sound to him. He didn't think he was neglecting his fields, but he did love this work. The timber seemed almost alive beneath his hands. Even as a *youngie*, still new to carpentry, he'd loved the smell of cut lumber, the solidness of the wood beneath his hands. He'd spent days in Abel Glick's wood workshop, learning all he could.

He smiled. Those had been good childhood days: the running wild in the afternoons after the trial of poring over his books. None had been more glad to have finished schooling when it was done. His *Geschwischder* had roamed the fields, too, as *youngies*, but none of his brothers and sisters had been as much an adventurous boy as himself. Isaac's mouth quirked as he remembered how *verrickt* he'd been. Wild and rambunctious and full of energy.

If only he'd learned to see all the consequences of his actions...

Pushing the plane again over the board in his hands, the smile fell from his face. His father was right. Mercy Yoder was a good-looking woman. He just wished he'd had no hand in her current situation. Wished he'd never met Daniel Stoltzfus.

That fall a year back, Mercy's fiancé had come to Mannheim to visit family—a relative of the same Abel Glick who'd taught Isaac so much in the past before he'd fallen ill. Isaac had readily worked old Abel's fields, never thinking of the outcome of his working alongside Daniel.

Isaac had never intended Daniel to take him seriously that teasing night. Not really. Never thought the *Mann* would find the spark in Isaac's jokey bantering to leave this Amish life... Not even when the joking had turned into jeering. Daniel was hard to work with, but that didn't excuse Isaac's sin.

Two days later the screen door of Bontreger's general store in Mannheim closed behind Mercy as she followed her *Aenti* Martha inside, her footsteps echoing on the wood floor. The store served their small community, supplying everything the plain, simple folk couldn't trade for or make themselves. Mercy smiled at and exchanged smiles with an exiting young *Frau* she'd met at the meeting, but whose name she couldn't remember.

As she walked through along the shelves, she felt soothed by the sense of familiarity around the place. There was a store just like this at home in Elizabethtown that smelled of lemon juice and vinegar and fresh produce brought in from the farms nearby. As she examined a small area stocked with home remedies, she trailed her hand along the smooth wood shelf, barely registering the few others in the store. Back at the counter, her *Aenti* chattered with the store owner and his *Frau,* her shopping basket on her arm.

Still examining the tonics and ointments in the small section, Mercy stepped forward to the shelf to let a *Maedel*—a girl child— walk by behind her, her steps loud on the wood floor boards. Shifting back to her original position once she could, Mercy made a face at the small shelf area. Basic items, mostly. And nothing for the many ailments necessary to a hard life of getting crops from the soil. Many times, she'd used *Grossmammi's* peppermint lavender balm to ease *Daed's* body aches and yet there was nothing like that here.

Knowing *Aenti* Martha had a long list of goods to get—not counting her tendency to lengthy chats—Mercy meandered down the aisle, almost able to pretend she was back at home. She missed her own little town. Before Daniel's defection had laid her open to both the pity and censure of neighbors, home had been such a peaceful, loving place. It had never made any sense that she was somehow responsible for his choice, but still…

She wondered—and she knew others did as well—had she somehow caused him to leave?

At the end of a shelving row of pickled beets, rich red in their jars, Mercy saw an attractive beardless *Mann* standing at a closed door off to the side of the building, his shirt sleeves rolled up to show brown, muscled arms.

Isaac Miller.

"Sarah," he said to the closed door, in an urgent undervoice. "I can't hear you, *Liebling*. Open the door. Are you crying?"

Unmoving, Mercy watched him.

"*Bencil*. Sarah let me in." He leaned closer to the door, dropping his voice. "Are you alright? Why can't you come out of the restroom?"

All of a sudden, Mercy realized that the girl who'd walked past her must be the one now inside the restroom. She looked around the store to see if she could find the child's mother and alert her to the *Bencil* having a problem. The child might be sick.

The owners stood at the front counter, talking still to *Aenti* Martha, but the only other two women she could see—one over by the produce and one at the pickle barrel—were clearly too old to be the child's *Mamm*. A *Grossmammi* perhaps? There was no way to know and the *Maedel* was obviously upset about whatever problem she had.

Moving forward, Mercy stopped next to Isaac, peripherally aware that he was even more attractive than she remembered and smelled nicely of clean air and fresh wood. She had no idea who the child was to him, but she felt compelled to offer help.

"*Goedenmorgen,* Isaac Miller. May I be of help?"

Whipping his head around, a harassed look on his face, he said, "Oh. Oh, *yah*. Sarah, *Liebling*, a nice lady is here. A friend of mine. Will you talk to her? Tell her the problem?"

Blinking at her quick elevation to friendship, Mercy waited in silence, standing next to him by the door.

"You can't get my *Mamm*?" It was a feeble question.

"*Liebling*, you know she's too far away."

Standing at his shoulder, Mercy registered the warmth of his nearness and refocused on the tearful, childish voice on the other side of the door.

"My *Bruder*, Enoch's daughter," Isaac whispered over his shoulder to Mercy. "She won't come out and I don't know why!"

There was no answer as the girl, apparently, thought about his offer.

"Well," a small voice wavered through the paneled wood door. "Okay, I guess."

The door lock could be heard being pulled back, before she eased the door open a crack.

"My *Mamm* told me this would happen," Sarah said several minutes later, as she sat glumly on the closed toilet seat. "I just didn't... It's just..."

"I know," Mercy responded with sympathy, pressing her hand against the girl's skirt-covered knee. She squatted against the wall in the small restroom, remembering her own transition to womanhood. "Even when you know what to expect, it can be a total shock the first time. Does your tummy hurt, too?"

"Yes." Sarah heaved a great sigh. "I thought I was sick or had eaten something bad."

"Is the pad I gave you comfortable? I only had a couple of handkerchiefs, but your *Mamm* will have plenty of cloths just for this."

"Yes. I guess it's okay." The girl blushed as if realizing she sounded ungracious. "Thank you, Mercy. I didn't know what to do. I just thought I needed to use the restroom and then there was all this..."

"It can be scary." Mercy smiled. "Like you're dying or something."

"And I'm here with my *Onkle* Isaac..." She drew a deep breath, turning pink. "I just couldn't come out of the restroom. It's just so embarrassing!"

Mercy straightened in the small restroom, saying with bracing encouragement. "You have nothing to be embarrassed about, Sarah. It's a very natural thing that every girl goes through. But, of course, it's very private. Don't worry about your *Onkle* Isaac. I'll make sure he doesn't bother you about this."

Getting up slowly, Sarah said, "You can do that? Thank you, Mercy."

Leaning against the wall near the door, Isaac idly staring ahead as he mused about a kitchen shelving unit he was making for *Frau* Glick, now that her husband was no longer with her. It was the least he could do since he'd originally learned woodcraft from old Abel Glick.

Isaac had heaved a sigh of relief when Mercy Yoder slipped into the restroom with Sarah. Kate and Enoch often trusted him with the *youngie*, particularly now that Kate's hands were filled with caring for the *Boppli*, as well as Sarah, Enoch and the house. He certainly didn't want to do anything to lose their trust.

Spending some time mentally measuring the various bottles and jars on the store shelves and making note, so he could accurately build the Glick's unit, he was aware of murmuring voices coming from the restroom. At least, Sarah sounded less hysterical now. The realization cheered him.

After a half hour or so, the door beside him opened.

Isaac straightened from the wall to see Mercy come through the restroom doorway, followed by Sarah, her cheeks pink and her little black-*Kapped* head down.

With her hand on the girl's shoulder, Mercy said, "Sarah, why don't you go out and wait in your *Onkle's* buggy. I'm sure he'll be out in a moment."

The child murmured something that could have been agreement, hurrying down the store aisle to the door.

Standing next to the beautiful blue-eyed woman, Isaac watched his niece disappear.

Turning toward him, Mercy said briefly, "Don't ask her anything, Isaac Miller. Nothing. Do You hear me?"

"What? Nothing? Why?" he responded, confused. "If the *Liebling* is sick, I need to tell her *Mamm* and *Daed.*"

Walking with him towards the door, she said repressively, "Listen, Isaac. She's not sick. Don't even mention it to her. She'll tell her *Mamm* about it."

Mystified, he just shook his head.

She lowered her voice, giving him a significant look. "It's a *girl* thing. Don't mention it to her or she'll be terribly embarrassed."

"A girl thing?" Comprehension dawned. "Oh! A *girl* thing."

"*Yah*, a girl thing." Mercy repeated with emphasis as she waved at Sarah through the window, a reassuring smile on her face.

It hit Isaac all at once how embarrassing the incident would have been for the child and he reached out to shake Mercy's hand. "*Denki,* Mercy. You really helped. I won't say a thing. I'll act like it never happened."

"Good. See that you do. And goodbye." She turned to walk to where her *Aenti* Martha stood, still chatting at the counter.

He watched her walk away, reflecting on the fierce look she'd given him when she told him to say nothing to Sarah. So, the Amish princess had a kind heart? What would he have done without her?

It made him even more intrigued by the pretty woman...and guiltier about what he'd said to Daniel Stoltzfus.

Glossary of Amish Terms:

Boppli--baby
Daed--dad
Englischer(Englisch)
Danke—Thank you
Frau—wife
Gott—God
Kapp—starched white cap all females wear
Mamm—mom
Ne—yes
Ordnung—the collection of regulations that govern Amish practices and behavior within a district
Rumspringa—literally "running around", used in reference to the period when Amish youth are given more freedom so that they can make an informed decision about being baptized into the Amish church
Scholar—young, school-aged person.
Ya—yes
Youngies—adoleslenscents. Young people.

About the Author

Author Biography:

Rose Doss is an award-winning romance author. She has written twenty-seven romance novels. Her books have won numerous awards, including a final in the prestigious Romance Writers of America Golden Heart Award.

A frequent speaker at writers' groups and conferences, she has taught workshops on characterization and, creating and resolving conflict. She works full time as a therapist.

Her husband and she married when she was only nineteen and he was barely twenty-one, proving that early marriage can make it, but only if you're really lucky and persistent. They went through college and grad school together. She not only loves him still, all these years later, she still likes him—which she says is sometimes harder. They have two funny, intelligent and highly accomplished daughters. Rose loves writing and hopes you enjoy reading her work.

Amish Romances:

Amish Renegade(Amish Vows, Bk 1)
Amish Princess(Amish Vows, Bk 2)
Amish Heartbreaker(Amish Vows, Bk 3)

www.rosedoss.com
www.twitter.com - carolrose@carolrosebooks
https://www.facebook.com/carol.rose.author

91963805R00105

Made in the USA
Lexington, KY
27 June 2018